The Thoroughbred Conspiracy

by Robert Monahan

Lullabies
Lullaby Tiger Publishing

The Thoroughbred Conspiracy

by Robert Monahan

Copyright ©2000 Robert Monahan

Lullaby Tiger Publishing
3969 Hillside Dr.
Lexington, Ky 40514

Tel: 859 327 8291
Email: Prowriter@robertmonahan.net
Web Page: www.robertmonahan.net

ISBN 978-0-9838036-0-7

Cover Design by Sharon Bradley
www.sharonbradleydesigns.com

The Thoroughbred Conspiracy

by Robert Monahan

A sinister plot to control the Thoroughbred racing industry has hatched in the Middle East, and is destroying the equine bloodlines of Kentucky.

Is the villainous plot sounding the death knell for the horse racing industry?

Can the efforts and passions of Tucker Flannery, manager of Fairhaven Farm, and Doctor Gwendolyn Gardot, a research microbiologist with the Kentucky Equine Research Center, interpret the ravenous disturbance in time to restore the noble breed to its kingly reign?

A globe-trotting story of brotherly hatred,

revenge, murder, passion,

and

the overwhelming love of

horses.

This story is dedicated to the memory of the many individuals who have innocently lost their lives to the unmerciful acts of terrorism.

To their families and friends...

I am but a dream away

And humbly here await.

Your spirit as it calls for me,

Through time's suspended state.

Yet I shall live inside you

Where my love shall never end.

In tender waves of memory,

Until we meet again.

The Thoroughbred Conspiracy

Chapter 1

JFK International Airport - December 1995

The frigid wind whipped the powdery snow about the yellow and red luggage carrier, as it bumped and snaked its way across the tarmac toward the waiting 747. The dark eyed, olive skinned driver pulled the carrier just beneath the baggage door of the airplane. He was not an airport employee, but was hired by an agent of a wealthy Arabian prince. Among the luggage he placed into the cargo hold, was a small black bag, reminiscent of a time when doctors would make house calls carrying stethoscopes and medicines.

Not far away, a middle-aged priest stood waiting in the departure lounge, thinking about the declining health of a dear friend. Father Petrie knew in his heart that he'd earned this trip abroad, but was worried about the sickly, aging prelate Monsignor McSourley and the future of his parish. The atmosphere in the building was electric as he lost himself in the bustle of travellers, barely able to hear the tender weeping of a gray haired woman about to leave her two daughters, as she prepared to board Trans Atlantic's flight 718 bound for Rome. His own name over the loudspeaker startled him, interrupting his thoughts.

"Father Petrie, Father Francis Petrie please."

His senses peaked as he reached in his black suit jacket pocket for another Rolaids tablet. He'd been eating the antacids like candy ever since Monsignor McSourley had taken a turn for the worse. Walking to the ticket counter, he announced to the lady in charge, "Yes, I'm Father Petrie."

"You have an urgent call, sir. You may take it on the red phone."

He'd attended many a parishioner's bedside, over the years, and had been present for every kind of negative news one could possibly hear, but he dreaded taking the call.

"Hello, yes, this is Father Petrie."

"Dear God no!" His face pursed as he listened to Bishop Dunn relate the fact that Monsignor McSourley had just passed away.

"Father, is there anything I can do for you?" asked the kindly bishop.

"I'll return at once, the parish will need me. I, I'll have to attend to the arrangements."

"As you wish, my son. God bless you now."

Father Francis Petrie felt all of his 58 years as he slowly turned to the ticket agent cancelling his long overdue plans to vacation at the Vatican. Like most men of the cloth, he'd always put the needs of his parish ahead of his own, and this was not the time for him to deviate from that habit. As his luggage was unloaded from the plane's cargo hold, a small black bag, identical to his, came down the chute by mistake. Father Petrie's bag, containing gifts for the friends whom he'd planned to visit, would fly to Italy, while the mistaken bag was hastily thrown onto a luggage wagon and trucked back into the baggage handling area. Pitched onto a conveyor belt, it wound its way back from where it started, spilling down the revolving carousel to the distracted priest. With a tear-blurred glance at the numbers on his claim check, Father Petrie picked up the black bag along with his other luggage and made his way to the area gate. Walking through the automatic doors and out into the cold, noisy New York evening, his nostrils filled with the strong smell of jet fuel as he heard, "Help you sir?"

"Uh, yes, please, a taxi."

The tall man in a blue uniform waved for the next available cab in the departure queue. When the cab stopped, he placed the luggage into the front seat, as Father Petrie handed him a two dollar tip.

"Thank-you sir, and you have a nice day."

"Penn Central Station please," said the priest beginning his journey back home to St. Stephen's rectory in northern Philadelphia. He wept, openly, as thoughts of what he would say to the family and friends of his departed advisor flooded his mind.

As Father Petrie's cab sped away from the airport, a thin, middle aged cabin attendant made her way through the first class section of flight 718, welcoming the passengers on board. She stopped next to a dark, handsome man, lost in thought.

"Excuse me sir, would you like a magazine?"

"Thank you, no," said Sheikh Efram Al-Farouad, sovereign ruler of Karoumi, a country not far from Saudi Arabia and the eighth and newest member of the United Arab Emirates. Reclined in first class luxury he reflected on his visit to Chicago and L. A. and the connections he'd made in his quest to recruit the caliber of medical professionals necessary to build his hospital. He could have used his official plane for this trip, but he often travelled commercially, so as not to appear extravagant.

He listened with nervous anticipation to the whine of the four General Electric engines increase, as the monstrous machine roared down the three-mile ribbon of concrete. Climbing through the evening air, the plane banked eastward and flew into the twilight over the Atlantic. Efram marveled at the serenity of the late evening sky while he relaxed with a warm feeling that his life was under the clear direction of Allah. He was much like his father in that he wanted the best for his country and his people, but in sad contrast to his brother

Rajad, the younger of the two princes, and second in waiting for the throne. When Efram thought of Rajad, he felt culpable that he himself had become the favorite son and that Rajad had allowed himself to develop into an undesirable character.

Allowing his mind to wander, he could hear the engine noise fade into the slipstream of air rushing by at over four hundred miles an hour. He was faintly aware of the chatter of the people around him, a festive sound laced with the tinkling of ice cubes and the throaty laughter of a full figured woman seated directly across the aisle. Roused a second time from his dream-like state, he heard, "Excuse me sir, would you care for a cocktail?"

"Thank you, no."

His thoughts turned, once again, to Rajad as he tried to understand why his younger brother was so often in a hostile mood, cursing at him, provoking him into senseless arguments. Their father, Sheikh Ahmed Al-Farouad, loved both his sons dearly but was tied by royal tradition to groom the eldest as his successor. But, Efram took full advantage of his position whereby he often had Rajad followed so that he could report any of his illicit activities directly to their father. Although the Sheikh had known of most of Rajad's shortcomings, he could never bring to bear the discipline the younger boy so desperately needed. This was due to the fact that the Sheikh felt responsible for Rajad's mother's death when Rajad was so young.

Becoming rebellious and defiant, Rajad often ventured beyond the realm of good judgment a royal prince should maintain, socializing with people of common and even questionable stature.

As flight 718 gained cruising altitude, Efram's thoughts drifted back to the countless stories of one of the snitches he would employ to spy on Rajad, reporting to Efram any and all social infractions. The streets of Beladesh provided the perfect stage for a young man to hone a delinquent life-style. A place where succulent legs of lamb roasting over burning dung accompanied by the echoing notes of Muslim prayers wailing above dirty streets, that wanderlust could play to a standing room only crowd.

Efram remembered the call he'd received the night Rajad, then 14, and two of his friends were caught chasing a small herd of stollen goats through the village. A call was made to the palace constable whose job it was to relay any such message directly to Prince Efram who, in turn, relayed it to Sheikh Ahmed.

Efram recalled the young man with the large birth mark on the side of his face whom Rajad had befriended. The birthmark had earned him the nickname 'Darkside'. During their escapades, the young men would pilfer and vandalize the small city of Beladesh after which the prince would sneak back within the sanctity of the palace walls. Through Darkside, Rajad was introduced to a street smart dancer of 19 with whom he had been seen much too frequently until, in Efram's judgment, something had to be done.

Staring blankly out the window into the dark ocean, Efram could hear Rajad's anger reverberate through his memory as though it had occurred that morning.

"You had to tell him didn't you? Didn't you? You bastard," cursed Rajad through eyes of fierce black hatred.

He remembered his response as he wished he had not told their father.

"Rajad, my brother, it is for your own good. She was no one for you. Or for the family. She is a woman of the night and an embarrassment to us all."

"You bastard, you stinking bastard. Who are you to judge me or my friends?"

"Rajad, please. I only ask that you think of who you are. Your position within the family."

"Stay out of my life. I am the only one who can decide what is right for me."

"I am always on your side. I am your blood."

"That is by no choice of mine."

"Then think of our father. Think of our people."

"If you ever involve yourself in my affairs again Efram I swear. I,"

"You swear what? What will you do? Kill me? Is that what you are thinking? Rajad, I am always your brother."

"Well do not be this brother of mine. I do not need a brother like you. I do not need this, this BAD BLOOD!"

Efram knew that so much had happened since those early days, and that negative feelings had widened the gap between them, a burden which seemed always on his mind. He begged Allah to soften his younger brother's heart and allow the wealth of their brotherly good fortune to flow unimpeded through their lives.

Efram's thoughts turned to his father, and how he could ever replace the man who, for so many years, was his hero, his confidant, his mentor. These thoughts dominated his mind as he drifted off to sleep, while the Atlantic Ocean heaved and rolled 34,000 feet below. It was another five hours to Rome.

Chapter 2

The Bluegrass of Kentucky - Three months later

Tucker Flannery, one hand on the steering wheel and the other trying to keep a cardboard box containing two large styrofoam cups of coffee from spilling onto the seat of his Ford pickup, sped along the back roads of Kentucky, well within the heart of Thoroughbred country. It was a special night as Kissin Kouzins, winner of the Winston Challenger Cup and over $350,000.00, was in foal to Heart Lancer, stallion of the year in 1992 and 1993. Tuck had watched this horse grow from birth and, as manager of Fairhaven Farm, was in a hurry to be by the side of his prized mare. As the truck pulled into the lot behind the foaling barn, the late March night, thick with chilly damp fog, permeated Tuck's sleeveless jacket.

"Hey Doc, how's it looking?"

Doc Baich, retired veterinarian, horse lover and close friend of Mrs. Audra Marcum Blevins, owner of Fairhaven Farm, was kneeling at the hind-quarters of the laboring brood mare.

"Hell if I know, sure looks weak from here."

They had detected a faint heartbeat, but knew by the way the mare was carrying the foal that the offspring was not completely healthy. Kissin Kouzins, soaked with sweat and nearing exhaustion, nickered gently as Doc Baich grabbed the legs of the offspring protruding halfway through her birthing canal. Tuck went to the mare's head and began stoking her cheek, offering what little support he could.

"Come on now," said Doc Baich. "Just a little further. That's it. There ya go now, easy does it."

And with a final push and a weary groan, Mother Nature shook loose her newest Thoroughbred charge.

"Ohhhh Shhhhhit," said the doctor, in a sorrowful voice. "Looks like we got us another one. Damn!"

It was the fifth straight foal death that week and Tuck was angry. There appeared to be an overabundance of stillborn foals in Central Kentucky, and Tuck, as well as other members of the breeding industry, were alarmed. Something had infected the best of the breed and was wreaking havoc on the most talented Thoroughbred lineage in racing history.

Tuck called Carney Puckett, Fairhaven's head trainer, who'd spent the previous night at Turbalinda Farm where a seventh consecutive foal of Royal Thunder's had been stillborn.

"Looks like we got a frigin virus around here. Damn, the only one we got that's worth anything don't weigh 70 pounds," he barked into the phone to Carney. A newborn Thoroughbred should weigh on the average between 95 to 120 pounds and should gain its legs within sixty to ninety minutes following birth.

"Dammit, this thing's outta control. Dammit! Hang on!"

Tuck turned to Doc Baich, "Doc, what about that friend of yours from the research center, that biologist. She ever call you back?"

"Nope, not yet. Whadayasay we give her a call?"

Gwendolyn Gardot, a 38 year old microbiologist employed at the Kentucky Equine Research Center, awoke to the sound of her phone ringing on the table beside her bed.

Not this early, she thought. Her life had become a nightmare ever since this thing with the newborns had started, and she knew if she didn't have an answer soon, there would be hell to pay.

She was a slight woman, but all business when it came to her work.

Please Lord let this be some good news. "Hello," she said, in a sleepy voice.

"Gwen, Doc Baich here. I'm over at Fairhaven and, hell Gwen, we've got another one," his voice dropping to a tone beyond sadness.

"Not Kissin Kouzins?"

"Yeah, Gwen, this thing's bad. Real bad. Have you found anything?"

"Doc, the only thing I can tell you right now is that we're doing everything we can."

"Give me that," said Tuck grabbing the phone out of the doctor's hand.

"Doctor Gardot, this is Tucker Flannery. I'm the manager of Fairhaven Farm. What the hell are you people doing over there?"

Startled, and not used to being addressed in that tone of voice, Gwen fired back, "I can assure you, we are doing everything we can to resolve this situation."

"Situation! Is that what you're calling it, a situation?" Tuck looked at Doc Baich and snarled, "Now they're calling it a situation."

"Well, we've got more than a goddamn situation here missy!"

Having been under extreme pressure ever since becoming involved in this puzzling dilemma, she was quick to respond.

"Believe me, you're not telling me anything I don't already know," her voice somewhere between angry and professional.

"Well, when can WE expect to know something?"

"The moment I know myself."

Tuck knew he had no right to take his frustration out on Doctor Gardot like that, and in a split second, felt ashamed.

"Okay, I uh, well look, thanks. I'm sorry. Guess I was just," Tuck handed the phone back to Doc Baich and stormed out of the barn.

Chapter 3

The noisy news room reeked with the smell of ink as the presses located on the floor below spun their nightly run. Johnny Stone, sports writer for the Lexington Herald Leader, was placing the final touches on his daily column when his boss and editor, Sam Stroub, stuck his head in Johnny's tiny cubicle. Moving the clutter from the guest chair, the tall man sat down swinging his feet up on the edge of the cramped desk nearly knocking over a blue coffee cup with the words 'Big Blue' italicized in white. Sam was well over six feet when he stood up straight and had wisps of gray hair he'd let grow too long in a feeble attempt at covering his mostly bald head.

"So, what's up?" asked the energetic boss.

"Those bastards think they own the world, well screw 'em!" Said Johnny through twisted lips.

A cagey, sometimes brilliant reporter, Johnny'd been investigating the rumors of 'sponging' at a racetrack in northern Kentucky, when he'd heard something that piqued his curiosity. A stillborn horse or two is not significant news, but three on one farm in the same day was worth his attention.

"Now look, don't let that attitude of yours get us into any more trouble, you with me?"

"Hey, I call 'em as I see 'em. Isn't that what you pay me for?"

"Yeah, but don't get too cute. Dammit, those folks can buy and sell us, and I don't need to fight any more of your goddamn battles."

"Then let me follow the Wildcats, or have you got too many round-ball junkies already?"

The University of Kentucky Basketball Program may have been the biggest show in town, but Sam knew that when it came to following and reporting on the ponies, no one could hold a candle to Johnny Stone.

"You ought to be damn glad I like you so much, or I'd fire your lousy ass."

"Sure ya would, right after your frontal lobotomy."

Johnny was cocky and a darn good reporter, but he was walking a fine line with some of the articles he'd been writing. The racing industry, and especially the horse owners, did not want to read about 'sponging' any more than they wanted to see a fresh outbreak of Japanese Encephalitis.

'Sponging' is the placement of a small sponge inside a horse's nasal cavity to impair the animal's breathing while running, causing a slower racing speed, and, in some cases, death. Johnny didn't enjoy reporting this activity, but there were rumors. New rumors. Rumors of an infection.

Every good reporter has a news-worthy source of information or two, and Johnny enjoyed his share of folks he considered in-the-know. People who live for the opportunity of being the first to provide information to someone they know will print the scoop. With what he'd been hearing lately, that's just the way he was thinking of headlining his latest column... **Rumors of an Infection. Something is killing the Thoroughbreds.**

He knew that publishing a story like that would be ill received, as people in the equine industry tended to abhor negative press. He also knew it was a simple matter of money because, in the gambling world, untold millions of dollars are spent on everything from state lotteries to cock fighting. The horse racing industry, wanting its fair share, shakes in fear when a negative story emerges.

"Johnny, you know that's pretty bold. Are you sure about all this?" asked Sam.

"What do you need, a magnifying glass? This sucks and we're right in the middle of it. Hell we gotta print it!"

"You know, I really don't like this one. Don't get me wrong, I want the story as bad as you do, but I don't want us to be the culprits who always print rumors."

"Neither do I, but since when did that ever stop us? Hell, we've been on the front end of just about every big story in town."

"Yeah, but most of that's university or sports related. This is different. We're talking about big, big money, and the livelihood of most of the state. And we don't have any of the facts. I mean what would become of the Bluegrass if we didn't have this industry?" Sam's voice was growing morbidly soft.

"Wait, wait, now hold on here, where you going with this? Maybe I should hold things a few days, give myself a chance to think about it," said Johnny, pensively.

"I think you should. Why not get out amongst the devil and see what you can dig up. Maybe talk to some of the farm folk. Hell, you know those people."

"Yeah, well. I'm not all that popular right now. Hell, with all this 'sponging' crap that's been going on, these folks won't be exactly glad to see me."

"Just consider it a chance to get away from your desk for a few days. You could use a break, couldn't you?"

"I guess so. Okay tomorrow I'll be out and about, so don't be looking for me all day wanting me to write some not-shit article to bail you out at the last minute."

"Who me? Would I do a thing like that?"

Ordinarily Johnny would retaliate with something equally sarcastic, but he just sat motionless, his chin in his hand, staring at his computer.

Chapter 4

She was walking up to the foaling barn looking as though she hadn't slept in a week, when Tuck caught sight of her.

"Help ya, ma'am?" asked the boy from the stall just behind her.

"Can you tell me where I might find Tucker Flannery?"

"That's me," said Tuck walking toward her carrying a warming blanket.

"Mr. Flannery, I'm Doctor Gardot, we spoke on the phone."

"Oh yeah, thanks for coming, but I sure wish we didn't have to meet under such circumstances."

I wish we didn't have to meet under any circumstances, she thought. Feeling that he'd been inappropriate with her on the phone, she wasn't exactly in a very good mood.

I've had to deal with assholes all my life, and he's just another in a long, never-ending line.

She'd prepared herself for an argument and was going to give this pompous ass a piece of her mind, but was sidetracked by the horseman's approach. Looking her square in the eye and with a shyness in his voice he stuck out his right hand saying, "I'm sorry I was so gruff on the phone Doc. I ah, I'm not usually like that. It's just that this problem we're having's gotten to me, but I should never have talked to you like that, I apologize. I was out of line."

Damn! She thought, *just when I was beginning to really dislike this guy, he had to go and say a thing like that.*

Collecting herself, she asked if she could examine the foal.

"You bet, he's right over here."

Leading her through the breezeway, they walked down the shedrow to a stall on the backside of the barn.

"We left him just like you asked, we didn't clean him, up or nothing, just threw that tarp over him."

She could tell by Tuck's voice that he was truly saddened by the death of the foal. She readily identified with the situation, having lost a foal of her own when she was a child.

At first glance the little stillborn looked pitifully small and underweight. Although she had no way of weighing the animal in the barn, she knew that he couldn't weigh more than 60 pounds. She felt the skin and muscles for nodules or anything that might give her some clue. With a small flashlight and probe she examined the ears, nostrils, mouth, tongue and anal orifice. Although there were no bruises, she noticed that hair was missing in several places, as if it had been pulled out in clumps. The skin was black and bluish, indicating that blood had coagulated under the surface. The gum tissue was a dark red signifying that the foal had died from a lack of oxygen probably within hours of birth.

"I'd like to take him back to the lab with me."

"Sure, sure. I'd appreciate it you'd call me when you know something."

"Certainly. It may take a few days though."

She was beginning to feel more comfortable around the man who, the day before, had yelled at her over the phone.

"No problem. I'm not going anywhere."

Looking at her with sincerity and sadness he said, "You know, we gotta fix this thing, Doc. Whatever it is."

"Yeah, I know. I wish I could tell you something Mr. Flannery, but at this point I don't have an answer."

"Please, call me Tuck. And I understand. You seem like someone who hates stillborns as much as I do."

"I grew up with a horse of my own so yeah, I do. I'm more comfortable inside a barn than I am in my own home." *If I had a home*, she thought. *If I had a life. I just need to get out more,* she surmised.

Living in a two bedroom apartment on the south side of Lexington she'd tried to make a nice home, but something always seemed to be missing.

"You from around here?" he asked, shyly.

"I'm from Texas originally. That's where I grew up anyway. I was raised on a farm just outside Lockhart. My grandmother had a few acres and I had my first horse when I was nine."

"I've never been there. Shoot, I've hardly been outta Kentucky."

"Mind if I examine the mare?"

"No, not at all. We took her back to her stall this morning. Didn't want the foal's scent to rile her."

They talked as they walked the quarter-mile over to the mare's barn, both noticing they not only shared common interests, but felt at ease with one another. Arriving at the mare's stall, Gwen examined the animal giving her a wide birth.

"Well, she looks sound to me. I'm going to take some blood and tissue samples, but this gal seems pretty healthy. Doesn't look like she's been affected at all. Whatever killed her baby doesn't appear to have bothered her."

"That's what Doc Baich said. It's the dangdest thing he's ever seen."

"So, have you known Doc Baich long?"

"Just about all my life. He was a friend of my dad's. He's quite a guy."

"Yeah, we think a lot of him over at the research center, too."

"I've always admired the way he loves the horses. He's retired and he still comes around during foaling season and gets right in there. He won't take any money, though. He and Mrs. Blevins are good friends. Yeah, ya just can't beat ol' Doc Baich."

Gwen took samples of blood and urine and swabbed the mare's nose, tongue, vagina and anus before looking for telltale signs of additional disease or distress. The mare's eyes responded properly to light and her coat was smooth and full.

Her muscles seemed sound as well as her legs and hoofs. She had no trouble breathing, nor was her heart rate abnormal. Her temperature was within range for her size, and she had eaten a healthy ration of oats within hours of dropping the foal.

"Well, I guess I better get back to the lab," said Gwen.

The horse's corpse, covered with a dark brown tarp, was placed in the back of Gwen's pickup truck, as she climbed in behind the steering wheel before turning to Tuck.

"Thank you Mr. Flannery, I hope I'll be calling you real soon, and I hope I can give you some good news."

"Thank you Doctor, I hope you will too. And I hope we can meet again on better terms."

"That would be my pleasure."

Tuck walked back to the small office at the center of the foaling barn, his thoughts consumed with the woman he'd just met. His thoughts were fleeting, however, he had mares in foal.

The basement of the Kentucky Equine Center contained several sterile rooms where everything from autopsies to experiments were performed which was where Gwen had placed the remains of the dead horse. Upon her arrival she immediately focused her attention on cutting up the horse's carcass, as her mind was awash in puzzlement.

I don't get it, she thought. *Several things are consistent with various diseases, but collectively are inconsistent with anything I recognize.*

She'd collected samples of the horse's hair, skin, tongue, muscle, heart, brain, colon, stomach, liver and spleen, and was placing them in sterile plastic bottles when Dr. Frederick Radabaugh, director of the Livestock Disease and Diagnostic Center, called.

"Working kinda late aren't you Gwen?"

"Yeah, I've just cut up another stillborn."

"And?" his voice sounded anxious.

"I've never seen anything like this. I'm guessing, but, it's almost like EIA. I mean a mutant strain or something, but how it could infect a newborn, I have no clue."

Equine Infection Anemia, or EIA, is a virus which is thought to be transferred by blood-feeding insects. Although not considered directly contagious, EIA can cause chronic infection and recurrent fever.

"I'm calling a meeting first thing in the morning, Gwen and I want you there. Please be in my office at eight sharp."

She finished cleaning the table and placed the samples under refrigeration before driving home. Glancing at the mail she fell into bed realizing that tomorrow was going to be another grueling day.

Chapter 5

University of Kentucky Equine Research Center

It was 8:45 and the mood in the large conference room on the second floor of the research center was electric although smelled of fresh-brewed coffee. Physicians and doctorate level scientists of varying animal backgrounds were anxiously awaiting the results of the previous day's analysis of the horrific equine malady that had invaded the horse farms. A large oval table near the center of the room was surrounded by several large comfortable chairs. Along the walls hung pictures of famous Thoroughbreds whose lives the equine facility had saved.

"All right, may I have your attention, please, we've got a lot to do this morning," said Dr. Radabaugh. "As most of you know, we've had several problems with newborns in the area, most of which have been stillborn, and we can't seem to put our finger on the problem. So far we've autopsied five in the last few days and, although we've seen some signs of what appears to be anemia or infection of one type or another, no one thing has surfaced as a common contributor. Doctor Gardot performed the most recent cut last night; Gwen, why don't you tell us what you found?"

Gwen took the podium with confidence, her data assembled neatly in front of her.

"The latest foal death yesterday morning, was a male out of Kissin Kouzins from Fairhaven Farm weighing approximately 57 pounds. Most major organs including the heart, lungs, kidneys and spleen were significantly under developed. The hair was missing in several places and the skin was blotched over 40% of the body in a dark brown color."

Roger Pulliam, a fifth-year graduate student was performing his own differential diagnosis as Gwen rattled off her findings. Roger was 25 years old and had just failed his first attempt at earning his doctoral degree, largely due to his unfavorable attitude and cavalier dismissal of the details of departmental protocol. He interrupted Gwen with one of his many untimely questions.

"What about the mare?"

Tired and a bit cranky from a string of sleepless nights, Gwen held up her hand like a traffic cop saying, "I'll get to that."

Roger, unburdened with an overabundance of patience, asked again, "Did you examine the mare?"

"Roger please," said Dr. Radabaugh, quickly. "Let her finish."

Radabaugh didn't necessarily like Roger, but he knew the energetic young man possessed one of the finest minds in the room. Whenever one of the computers in the department had a bug, and lately there had been several, Roger was the first person called. His main problem was that he couldn't tolerate office politics. In the world of research at the university level, office politics cannot be regarded as a spectator sport. Roger not only refused to play, he refused to pay. His sour attitude was redeemable mostly because of his uncanny ability to support his compatriots with an inexhaustible supply of facts. He wasn't always liked, but he was definitely respected, and Dr. Radabaugh, though unhappy with Roger's shortcomings, considered himself fortunate to have this bright young man on his staff. Gwen presented the facts in meticulous order, and was careful not to taint the data with her own suspicions and opinions.

"I did examine the mare and found her to be completely sound. Her vitals were fine, and she looked good for just having produced a stillborn."

"Did I not hear that this is consistent with the other deaths, that the mares have all presented this way?" asked one of the scientists in attendance.

"Now wait a minute, are you telling me that none of the mares have been found to be contaminated? No signs of infection?" asked Dr. Radabaugh.

"I believe so," said Gwen.

"Maybe we should double check this," said one of the epidemiologists invited to the meeting.

"Who's the daddy?" asked Roger.

Although no one appreciated the way Roger had asked the question, all eyes and ears remained on Gwen for the answer. She was caught off guard, but didn't hesitate.

"I don't know."

"Maybe we ought to look at him," said Roger.

"That's not a bad idea," said the only reproductive physiologist in the room. "What about the stallions?"

Dr. Radabaugh quickly responded. "Gwen, can you find out who the sire was and Roger, can you work with Gwen on this? Also, we need a team to recheck the mares. I want every mare examined before we meet again."

"Anyone heard of anything going on anywhere else?" Dr. Radabaugh looked around the room, then directly at Roger. "What about the Internet?"

"I'll check, but if anything's happening, no one's talking about it. Maybe I should make a few phone calls."

"No way. If this is local, we've got to get on top of it before we alert the world. We consider ourselves the best in this business people, and this is no time to disprove it."

"Now wait a minute Fred," said Dr. Marion Tramlecki, a 56 year old parasitology expert with thirty-plus years experience. "What if it isn't local? We have a responsibility here."

"I agree, but let's be a little knowledgeable about what we're responsible for first," said Dr. Radabaugh.

"Why not just see what's out there? I mean why not make a few phone calls, just to test the water?" asked Roger.

"I like the way Fred thinks," said Dr. Tramlecki. "We don't want to alert the world if we don't know what it is we're talking about. Think about it."

It was clear they were divided on the issue, but after a lengthy discussion, they all agreed to postpone any activity which would alert the equine community, unnecessarily.

"Okay, that's it, we meet here every morning at eight sharp, until this thing is solved. I don't want any more foals dying. Let's also watch where we send these samples. Folks, if we can't find it in our own backyard, we're in the wrong business. And I sure don't want the newspaper printing anything. No sense them starting something we can't finish."

Immediately following the meeting, Gwen was on the phone with Tuck to obtain the name of the sire of the most recent stillborn.

"Mr. Flannery, this is Doctor Gardot. Who was Kissin Kouzins bred to?"

"Hi Doc, let's see now, that was Heart Lancer."

"Where is he standing?"

"Well, he's one of ours, but he's over at Stallion Manor right now. Hell Doc, he's one of the best."

Stallions may stand at different farms for a variety of reasons, such as breeding facilities, joint ownership, or location of the mares.

"I'd like to examine him."

Tuck's heart sank, realizing that the research center was no closer to a solution.

"Sure, sure, I don't see a problem. I don't know his schedule offhand, but we should be able to work something out. Whadya have in mind?"

"How about two this afternoon?"

Tuck's mind raced. He'd never even thought there might be a problem with the stallion, but then again he was no doctor. He wondered if this was just a stalling tactic, or if the problem really could have come from the stallion. He didn't know the horse's schedule, but quickly realized the importance of the examination. If it was Heart Lancer's fault, Tuck would need to prevent any further breeding.

"Okay, what if I meet you there?"

"I'll see you at two then."

Chapter 6

Karoumi - The United Arab Emirates

In the Islamic world, a woman's place is in the home, and her primary responsibility is raising children. Although in modern times some Islamic countries, including Karoumi, allow and encourage women to work outside the home, provided they are afforded the appropriate respect; this was not the case in 1967. Among the many issues before him, Sheikh Ahmed Al-Farouad pondered the role of Karomi's women.

Raised with the lineage of responsibility like the generations before him, he understood that it was the burden of responsibility which allowed him to rule with patriarchal understanding. Identifying with this from early adolescence, as though it were genetically parsed into his soul, it wasn't until he'd reached his early forties that he'd become a student of his own spiritually decisive qualities, not only loved, but worshiped by the people he served.

His father, Sheikh Kalash Al-Farouad, was a tender disciplinarian, but sometimes displayed an egotistic attitude toward his tribe, creating several enemies. On one such occasion, a 14 year-old boy who'd been working in the slaughtering area, which at the time was nothing more than an open pit at the edge of town, was caught pilfering meat. Refusing the advice of the inner tribal council, Sheikh Kalash decided to remove the fingers of the boy's right hand. The boy, a bastard and therefore an outcast by local standards, had no representation among the men who decided his fate. Although an unpopular decision, Sheikh Kalash, seeking to improve his political standing through a demonstration of barbarous strength, ordered the punishment carried out. Unfortunately, he was unaware that his dictatorial act of butchery had set in motion his own karmic demise. Although embarrassed by his father's unwise action, Sheikh Ahmed always spoke of him with love and respect.

Determined not to follow in his father's footsteps, Sheikh Ahmed desired to lead his people with a logical mind and a compassionate heart. And in this harsh and desolate country, at the tender age of 19, a decade after the pearl industry had floundered and a decade prior to the oil industry explosion, Abu bin Ahmed bin Salemn Al-Farouad found himself at the head of a tiny tribal community on the southeastern border of Saudi Arabia. Along what was once known as the Pirate Coast. The year was 1952.

Aula bint Hamen bin Salehur Al-Klafern presented Sheikh Abu bin Ahmed bin Salemn Al-Farouad with two children within the first seven years of their marriage. Efram, born in 1957 and Rajad six years later. Although the home she made for her family was full of love and tenderness, the sheikh spent most of his time away, involved with the matters of state.

Within the sanctum of an Arabian tribe, young men enter manhood when they reach the age of 12 and are often encouraged to accompany the older men on hunting trips. It was on one of these excursions that Efram accompanied his father on a falconry expedition, leaving Rajad at home with his mother.

On the second morning following their departure, while Rajad was enjoying his breakfast, Aula felt the first pain.

"Aughh," she screamed, falling to the floor, knocking Rajad out of his chair. The frightened child had no idea that he was witnessing his mother's final moments.

"Ayeeeeee," she cried placing both arms up over her ears in a feeble attempt at squeezing the thunderous pain from her head. Thrashing about uncontrollably, the blood trickled then gushed from her nostrils and ears. Adrenaline poured into her bloodstream, causing her heart rate to increase in an effort to sustain her blood pressure, but nothing could stop the pain and no one could save her from the torturous ordeal. It was over in minutes as Rajad crawled on the floor next to his mother.

"Mamma," he cried, but to no avail. He lay in a fetal position next to her, clinging to her arm.

How long they remained in this fashion before being found was never disclosed. Upon hearing the news, the sheikh with Efram by his side, rushed to the infirmary where they viewed Aula's body one last time prior to burial.

Significantly affected by the suddenness of his wife's death, Sheikh Ahmed suffered a life-altering affliction that cast a pall of sadness over him he could not escape. His salvation was to become immersed in the leadership of his tribe, which, through the advent of the oil industry, had been steadily growing. On a warm summer morning in 1976, Karoumi became sovereign and was rendered the eighth Trucial State of the United Arab Emirates. A joyful crowd gathered to receive the words of their sheikh, their leader and modern-day prophet.

"Let every man within this country dare to dream, and then reach beyond himself to achieve that dream. We shall build this country together not only for ourselves, but for our children and their children." The applause was thunderous as the sheikh concluded his speech.

Mustafa Ramon Truchev, having spent the better part of the day shaking hands and politically posturing, decided to celebrate the royal occasion in a less colloquial environment. An official representative of the Turkish government, he was badly in need of refreshment, as he sought the serenity of a local bistro.

Palen Prahstomank moved her belly in and out to the rhythm of the music, stirring the imagination of several local patrons as Mustafa walked into the smoky bar flashing her a toothy smile. Tall and thin with large black eyes and a very tanned face behind a thick, black mustache, he'd dressed in a creamy white suit, handmade calfskin shoes, a pale yellow shirt and soft brown tie. Not well built, nor particularly handsome, he did possess the polish of a diplomat and the look of old world money. Carrying himself with savvy, and an air of confidence he looked like he not only owned the world, but could sell it at any price.

"Ouzo!" he snapped.

The drums played a pagan African beat as Palen shimmied and wriggled with the graceful movement of a five foot, four inch snake. Turning her attention to Mustafa she smiled as their eyes locked passionately. She was well proportioned, just the way he liked them, carrying a few extra pounds mostly in her round, plump buttocks and large, heavy breasts. Married for what seemed like an eternity to a woman who, due to her religious beliefs, had never allowed herself the joy and ecstasy of deep orgasm, Mustafa longed for sexual satisfaction.

Inviting her to his table and buying her several drinks, it wasn't long before they found themselves inside his lavish hotel room where their bodies meshed with the graceful abandon known only to those who challenge the laws of righteousness. Their lovemaking, on this their first night together, was indulgent and bountiful, and for the next several months whenever Truchev visited Karoumi, the two repeated this primal ritual until the day she announced to him that she was with child.

"What do you mean?" he roared in obvious displeasure. "How could this happen?"

Palen sat on the edge of the bed with her head buried in the silk scarf he'd given her on one of his visits. She was a worldly woman, but at this moment was without words.

"How do you know it is mine?" he demanded, in a viciously cold voice.

"I know," she said softly, tears falling from her beautiful black eyes. "I just know."

She'd fallen in love with him, despite his temperamental moods, and didn't know how to handle his verbal abuse.

"You know my position. How could you do this to me?"

After several moments of pacing and berating the helpless woman, Mustafa announced, "I can do nothing for you. Nothing!"

Storming out of her room, he hailed a cab to his hotel, packed his bags and arranged for the next flight back to Ankara, Turkey.

A pregnant belly dancer in a remote, religious Arabian community, doesn't have many options. After surveying the situation, Palen was persuaded to move in with her sister Kaspha, until the baby came. It was a tight fit in the small apartment, but Palen managed to endure by keeping mostly to herself through the long prenatal months. On one occasion she told her sister that she was thinking of going to Turkey to confront Mustafa.

"No! You cannot do that, he will have you shot."

"What life do I have here? Anyway, I believe he still loves me."

"He is a married man. He will not allow you in his life."

"I want it for my baby, so he won't be just a, a." Palen couldn't bring herself to say the word.

"Do not think about it now. Wait until the baby is born. You will think more clearly then."

She was seven months pregnant when she purchased a ticket aboard Turk Hava Yolari Airlines to Ankara. As the afternoon sun lit the crystal blue January sky, she walked the stone path to the M. Kemal Attaturk Government Complex, up the stairs to the central building where she found the main receptionist.

"I am looking for Mustafa Truchev."

"Mr. Truchev is in the Manor Complex, 6th floor, west wing, but, you must have an appointment."

"I've had an appointment for months."

Walking as best she could with the pain in her back from sitting uncomfortably on the plane, she made her way to the west wing of Manor Complex. Riding the elevator to the sixth floor, she marched through the main reception area and into the outer sanctum of her former lover's office.

"Is he here?" she demanded, loudly.

The elderly receptionist parked stoically behind a massive

desk looked at her and, with a heavy voice acquired from 40 years of unfiltered cigarette smoke asked, "Do you mean Mr. Truchev?"

"Yes, I mean Mr. Truchev. Mr. Mustafa Ramon Truchev, the father of this baby," she yelled, pointing to her stomach.

"I'll see if he is in," she said, flashing her eyes toward the politician's closed door. But with the quickness of a cat, Palen burst through the inner office door exclaiming, "I'll do that myself."

Taken completely by surprise, Mustafa blurted, "Palen, what are you doing? Why are you here?"

Walking toward the startled politician with her hands on her hips, she cut him off in mid sentence. "Don't! Don't even say it."

"Palen, Palen my darling."

"I am the mother of your child!" she yelled, spitting the words at him, speaking considerably loud so that everyone within range would make no mistake about her condition and his responsibility.

"I will not discuss this here. You will leave now. We will discuss this later."

"Oh no you don't. We will discuss this right here and now."

Maneuvering behind his desk, he placed the sole of his shoe over a small switch on the floor, sending a signal to security stationed in the basement. Within seconds three heavily armed guards burst into Mustafa's office as though the entire complex was under siege.

"Take her!" he commanded. "Take this woman away, she has threatened me."

Kicking and screaming, she hit one of the guards as they manhandled her out of the office and down the service elevator. Mustafa Truchev, not used to having his integrity challenged, washed his face from the sink in his private bath, fixed his tie, locked his desk and went home for the day.

Palen spent the next week in a Turkish prison after which

she was tried, found guilty and placed in the unofficial Turkish women's compound in Bursa. She, like so many women before her, would be required to work out her life as a confined prostitute until her death. The future she'd imagined for her unborn child was over.

Chapter 7

Karoumi - 1992

In striking contrast to Sheikh Ahmed's white flowing robes, Rajad dressed in a new blue suit he'd purchased for the formal meeting with his father. Entering the ornate office, the sheikh motioned for Rajad to take a seat across the large green and white alabaster table he used for a desk.

"My son, it is always a pleasure to see you looking so well. You have made a formal appointment with me, something you need never do. For what do I deserve such honor and respect?"

"Father, I have an idea I would like to share with you and greatly desire your wisdom and direction."

"I have been waiting a long time for this day. I am always willing to listen to your ideas."

Relaxing in his leather chair, the sheikh gave his son one of his many heartfelt blessings.

"May logic guide your thoughts and may the love of our people direct your desires."

Jumping to his feet, the prince appeared like an executive about to address the directorate board at General Motors. His enthusiasm for the subject overcame his nervousness.

"Father, I would like to build a research facility. A world class equine racing stable, here in Karoumi."

Hesitating briefly, he continued.

"A place for which our people could be proud. A place where a pure breed of animal could be developed. A place where dread diseases could be cured. Father, I want to build a world class equine facility."

The sheikh sat perfectly still allowing the idea to penetrate his finely tuned mind. Through the process of elimination and years of experience in royal leadership, he digested his youngest son's request. With a placid face and a voice devoid of emotion, the sheikh finally asked. "And how do you feel this will benefit our people?"

Anticipating his father's response, Rajad sprang to the center of the room, bursting with enthusiasm.

"They will benefit in many ways. First, Karoumi will be known worldwide as a place of healing and wellness. Secondly, the champion horses we develop will be the symbols of our land."

"And you feel our people need these symbols?"

"Not only do THEY need them, we ALL need them. Father, it is 1992, the Arabian horse that you were raised with no longer exists. It is only a dream. It has been over-bred for years. We could recreate it right here in Karoumi, for all the world to see. We could restore the breed to what it once was, what it should be. An icon, the master horse and," pausing momentarily, "the true symbol of our land."

The mood in the room thick with anticipation forced the sheikh to remain motionless. His son had an interesting idea, but something did not sit well with him. He believed what his son was saying had merit, but he also knew that associated with the development of horses was the element of gambling, something he firmly opposed. Gambling meant addiction and addiction meant poverty.

But the image of the master horse ran through the sheikh's mind like a breath of fresh air. He envisioned the beautiful mares and stallions, imagining the majestic offspring they could produce. He thought about how much he himself loved the animal. How he'd forgotten what a true symbol the pure Arabian stallion was to him and to all of Arabia. How pleasing were his thoughts of riding the wind on the back of the most prized creature in all of Allah's kingdom. The sheikh allowed his mind to wander for moments absorbing all that Rajad had said before speaking.

"My son. I am happy to hear you speak of this. I believe you have a sound idea. I would like you to develop a plan, hire a staff if you need, and when your work is near completion, bring it before the Municipal Council. I will tell you that I believe this is a much larger task than is appropriate for our country, but I am intrigued. I will pray for you and I hope you will be received well. However, I will not go against the council's decision. Whatever the council decides will be my decision."

The idea would have to be submitted to the various developmental committees for approval, but everyone knew, including Rajad, that if the sheikh gave it his blessing, it would be well received.

For the next several weeks, Rajad gathered a staff who worked diligently developing the plans for the design and construction of the (KERDC) Karoumi Equine Research and Development Center. Once in place, they forged ahead with plans for the (KETC) Karoumi Equine Training Center, which included a track, barns, pastures and all the associated facilities for training a world class breed of horse. Rajad lost himself in this task working around the clock until he was ready to present his plan to the Municipal Council.

Chapter 8

Children growing up within the confines of a Turkish prison compound suffer in many ways, most of which is carrying the label of bastard. A bastard child, by Middle Eastern standards, must live in constant disgrace, always wearing the sins of her or his parents like a socially degrading stigma.

The sky hung gray with the smoke from hundreds of coal and dung furnaces, as the steady drizzle of sleet made bitter the cold March morning. In the distance the wail of a Hindu devotee could be heard chanting the early melodic prayers atop a local minaret. It was the third Tuesday of the month as Palen brought forth a seven pound, six ounce baby boy who innocently enough was, at birth, a political prisoner. Babies born within the walls of a Turkish compound are examined by a physician, however facilities are extremely primitive.

A compound is a small village of buildings juxtaposed inside the confines of a wall-like prison with armed guards at each gate. The entire village is a brothel, serving citizens, government employees and tourists, allowing female prisoners to pay their debts to society by way of their sexual efforts. Rumor had it that a Turkish male citizen, guilty of a crime, could place a female member of his family in one of these compounds, in hopes of expediting or retiring his sentence.

"Here you are dear," said Jaima, a petty thief and drug smuggler from Crete, placing the baby in his mother's arms.

Exhausted from a seven hour delivery, Palen said softly, "He is so small, but he is so handsome."

"We have sent for the doctor, but who knows how long it will be. You must rest and try to eat something."

Palen placed the boy on her breast noticing a birth mark on

his left cheek that resembled a star. It was more a darkening of the skin than anything else.

I will ask the doctor, she thought falling into a dazed semi-consciousness.

Sasha Prahstomank did not eat much his first few days, but grew rapidly over the course of the next several months. He was a good boy becoming the delight of many of the women, always willing to aid with even the slightest of tasks until late one night, when he and his mother were mysteriously ordered to pack their belongings. With no time for good-byes they were sent to Karoumi aboard a Turkish DC3 military plane.

During his formative years Sasha became known to his street friends as Darkside, due to the birthmark on his cheek, which had grown darker than his olive tan skin. By the time he was 14 he was a hardened adolescent, afraid of nothing and no one, able to steal a street merchant blind while out maneuvering even the fastest policeman. Handsome and in perfect condition, he remained especially popular with several of the young ladies.

It was during his 17th birthday that he and Prince Rajad met one evening during one of Rajad's wild excursions. Under normal conditions these two young men would never have met, much less become friends, but Rajad was not a normal nobleman and Darkside was a friend to all.

Their nightly escapades fused a tight friendship. Developing a deep respect for one another, Darkside reflected the kinship of the brother Rajad wished he had, while Rajad inherited the brother for whom Darkside often dreamed. They shared their innermost feelings and on one such occasion Darkside told Rajad that he'd been thinking about returning to Turkey to confront his father.

"Why do you want to go through all that misery?" asked Rajad. "Do not be a fool."

"He is my father, I just want to look at him and," stumbling for words.

"He will have you hanged."

"I am his son! He will honor me as I do him."

"And how is it that he has shown his honor? After all these years, never even a letter? You will be nothing but a thorn in his side. He will gut you like a goat and throw you to the dogs."

"So be it! But he will know me. He will know that I exist and that I am someone. And I will have his name."

"You will have his name? You will have his shame, and he will not allow that. No, my friend, he will honor you by eliminating you. That is how he will show you his honor."

In the twenty years that had distanced Darkside from his birth place, Mustafa Ramon Truchev had become a widower. Retiring from public office he had moved to Yalova, a small town 120 kilometers from Istanbul.

On a warm September morning a taxi cab weaved its way through the heavy traffic from Istanbul's Yesilkoy International Airport, down through the crowded streets to the Galata bridge. Around every turn Darkside's olfactory glands met with a new and pungent smell. He'd lived at the poverty level all his life, and had grown accustomed to many a nasty experience, but could not believe the variance of stench a fascinating city like Istanbul could produce.

At the Galata bridge he boarded a ferryboat and sailed across the Dardenelle Straight, up along the Marmara Sea to the dock at Yalova. Leaving the boat, he walked behind the row of filthy buses parked amidst the people scurrying about, the men in their suit jackets and black big-apple woolen hats and the women in long, black overcoats with scarfs covering their heads. He didn't walk far before he found himself in front of a small but stately three-story house with a black iron fence and a beautiful rose garden.

When the manservant answered the door, Darkside, a picture of health, speaking broken Turkish, asked if Sir Truchev was at home. An elderly man walking with the aid of a cane inched his way into the front room. When their eyes met, Mustafa knew that his own flesh and blood was standing before him. Hugging the boy with gusto the old man made sure that his son was treated kindly for the entirety of his stay.

Following a brief visit and his pockets filled with money, Darkside was driven to the ferry landing and bid a warm good-bye from the man he knew would love and respect him as a son. With tears in his eyes he boarded the Istanbul ferry for his return to Karoumi.

He would now be able to tell Rajad, his mother and family that he had met his father, and was accepted by him. Feeling that he was finally a man of respect his thoughts were focused on changing his last name, when the ferry was waylaid by a Turkish gunship and boarded by six armed soldiers. When the military entourage exited the boat, there was one passenger missing. Darkside, hands cuffed behind his back, begging to know what was happening, was taken aboard the gunship and spirited away to a prison in Istanbul.

"Why? What have I done?" he demanded, but to no avail. No one could help him now. No one except his father.

It was over quickly, his arrest and trial. Then, following a short trip across the Bosphorus to the Asian side of Istanbul, he was placed in solitary confinement. It was clear that his father, the consummate politician, had set him up.

But why, he thought. *Why would he do this to me?*

Chapter 9

After days of sitting alone in a dank cell, Darkside's mind fell into a meditative trance where he began to visit some of the more pleasant memories of his youth. He remembered, fondly, the first time he was introduced to Prince Rajad following their argument over some boyish misunderstanding. He recalled that Rajad, used to having his way, tried to pull rank on him. Smiling, he relived the moment that he took control of the situation.

"Not here!" he recalled saying with a look on his face that said **I'm The Boss**! With a quick shove he had Rajad eating out of his hand.

How did I ever make that prince come my way, he thought. He remembered that he always respected Rajad's power, but was unafraid of it. Relaxing into his thoughts, he felt peace in the knowledge that Rajad, the Prince of Karoumi, had befriended him.

After the first week in solitary with no blanket or bed, Darkside was placed in a cell near two other political prisoners, both serving lengthy sentences for crimes that no one could substantiate. During his first year behind bars, he managed to gain the confidence and respect of his fellow inmates. He was pleasant in his conversation, despite the circumstances, and was often found in deep meditation. His only enemies were the guards, especially Nazr, who, from time to time, would drag him from his cell and force him to perform sexual favors. Nazr, nicknamed 'The Nazi', was the worst of the guards.

He especially enjoyed raping the prisoners while holding plastic bags over their heads. The frightful movements of a man gasping for breath and dying from lack of oxygen, brought Nazr extreme sexual pleasure. He also enjoyed placing the end of his lit cigarette between the buttocks of a helpless prisoner tied and bent over a hot metal table. Or clubbing the feet of one who's legs had been manacled in such a way as to allow the soles of his feet to be beaten with a large, flat club.

When Nazr would torture Darkside the debaucherous reprobate would place him in solitary confinement for several days so as to allow the hot-tempered Arab time to cool off. This activity went on for months until one morning when Darkside's cell door was pushed open, blinding his sensitive eyes.

"Sasha Prahstomank, step forth and follow me," ordered the guard.

Where are they taking me? he wondered, as he stumbled from the cell.

Shuffling behind the guard, his feet and hands chained together, he followed as best he could through the maze of dimly lit corridors, until he and the guard reached the front of the prison and a small room containing only a chair. The air was stagnant and foul, like an old museum. Standing in front of the guards, a pitiful sight, he noticed the ugliness of his surroundings - the walls, dirty and badly in need of paint. He wondered if this was the end.

Am I going to be hanged or shot, or even worse, tortured to death?

The prisoners only speculated on how capital punishment was carried out, they never knew for sure.

The leg irons and metal rod that held his elbows clamped painfully behind his back were removed and he was told to get dressed, as one of the guards threw an old green uniform and a pair of filthy boots at him. The arthritic pain in his elbows and shoulders brought a nasty tasting bile from his stomach to his mouth. He knew that vomiting would only cause the guards to beat him, so he choked down the disgusting fluid.

Pulling on the rotting, sweat-stained shirt and matching

pants, he pushed his feet into the cold, sock-less boots as his mind raced. *This must be how I am to be buried.*

From there he was marched to the front gate and shoved out into the warmth of the afternoon air, his eyes burning with sunlight, an experience he had all but forgotten. Picking himself up, he heard the large metal prison door clank behind him. Utterly astonished, he stood alone breathing the sweetness of freedom.

He didn't see the old Chevrolet pull up beside him. As the passenger door flung open, an unfamiliar voice, barked, "Get in, we must hurry!"

Darkside was blissfully unaware that his only true friend, a friend with the political clout and essential wealth necessary to release him from his damnable existence had come to his rescue, and had given him back his life.

Falling into the back seat, he could hear the endearing sounds of the city off in the distance as he breathed deeply, taking in all the sweet smells and fresh aroma of freedom.

Chapter 10

The immaculate royal conference room seemed to vibrate with energy as it swelled with the board members of Karoumi's Municipal Council. In the center of the room stood a large oval table surrounded by several matching leather chairs each occupied with either a member of the council or one of the sheikh's trusted allies. Sheikh Ahmed was the last to enter the room, walking to the head of the table before introducing his son to the gathering.

With the undivided attention of everyone in the room, Rajad stood, nervously, before the attendees clutching a pointing device in his hand. Moving between two overhead projectors and an enormous cardboard model of the proposed facility, he began his presentation.

"You will see gentleman, as I have outlined, Karoumi will become a world leader in the development of the new and improved Arabian horse. The true Arabian horse. And we will become the world's leading research center for the care and cure of equine diseases."

He remained the picture of confidence, as he presented his plan to the members of the council and the sheikh. He knew that staffing the research center would attract several professional people to Karoumi and that, eventually, the facility could become a great financial success. The architects, engineers and members of the municipality had worked, feverishly, to develop the overall plan, and it had come together in record time. The sheikh, although somewhat reserved, could not disguise his happiness. He'd hoped that Rajad would learn to work together with his brother Efram and, if this was any indication of things to come, he was sure it would happen. Determined to support his younger son he had decided to give him a chance.

The members of the council questioned Rajad and his staff for over an hour, and perceiving no negative responses, the sheikh nodded toward his son before ending the meeting with a proposal.

"It is settled then, the construction of an equine research center will begin immediately, as well as the development of a training center. Rajad will remain in charge of the project and will solicit the funds to complete the task."

"I am impressed," said the sheikh as the council members filed out. "You have done well, my son."

It was Efram who did most of the hiring when it came to staffing the schools, hospitals and municipal facilities, but it was now up to Rajad to acquire the doctors and scientists who would bring life to his research center. He toyed with the idea of soliciting Efram's help, but decided against it. If Efram could score a 90, he would score 100.

It wasn't long before the town of Beladesh was alive with the sounds of heavy construction. With a plethora of workers from all over the world, the Karoumi Equine Research Center was built in record time. Rajad had become a new man in the process, having matured nicely, much to his father's pleasant surprise.

Within six months of completion, a letter was sent to the director of every equine health, research and sport facility world-wide, that could aid in the development and growth of the Karoumi Equine Research Center. Among them were Auburn University, The University of California, The Maxwell H. Gluck Equine Research Center, Cornell University's Equine Research Park, The Kentucky Equine Research Center, The McPhail Laboratory at Michigan State University, and the Northwest Equine Reproduction Lab at the University of Idaho, to name a few. It read...

The Sovereign State of Karoumi, and eighth Trucial State of the United Arab Emirates proudly announces the development and construction of the Karoumi Equine Research and Development Center. Our mission is to build the finest equine facility in the world.

The people of Karoumi, under the explicit direction of Prince Rajad Al-Farouad, plan to recruit and staff the research center with professionals from the entire global equine community.

We are presently receiving applications in all areas of equine research. If this is of interest to you, please contact us at your earliest convenience.

My sincerest gratitude,

Sheikh Ahmed Al-Farouad

Within a matter of days, the equine world was notified that an opportunity for travel and professional development was available for individuals interested in furthering their careers. It was an exciting time and Karoumi was rapidly becoming the place to be.

Chapter 11

Dr. William Leach, head of the research facility at Montbalm Laboratory near Heath Virginia was just concluding his preparation for an evening lecture when he received a call from his old friend, Dr. Meredith Pehlagrem, Director of Equine Services at the Morgan Equine Research Center just east of Nashville.

"Hey Meredith, how are you?"

"Fine Bill, just wanted to know if you've heard about the positions over in the Gulf?"

"Oh yeah, I've heard. Sounds interesting. Course Lauren wouldn't go, but I've been thinking about it. She can stay here and do the entertaining while I'm gone."

It was no secret that Bill and Lauren Leach were not in love, nor had they ever been, and their marriage was hanging by a thread. She was a Wainscott who had come from old-south money, and was quite the socialite when she and Bill met during their undergraduate years. Her grandfather had discovered oil in Western Oklahoma earlier in the century, and had developed a prosperous plantation in Georgia. Bill and Lauren dated for three years after which they were married in one of the largest weddings in southern history. Bill often remarked that he thought the ordeal reminded him more of the *Gone With The Wind* movie production.

He was only twenty-six at the time, and had spent most of his college years engrossed in a medical library. But that was thirty years ago and since Lauren had not been blessed with any bouncing offspring, Bill's attention was always on the horses. He'd been wanting, for years, to test his doctorate mettle and broaden his horizons, but hadn't found the right niche. He was toying with the idea of going to Karoumi, when

Dr. Pehlagrem called.

"What about you, Mere?"

"It sounds adventurous, don't you think? I have to admit, I've been thinking about it too."

Dr. Meredith Louise Pehlagrem was a Harvard University graduate who'd earned her Doctorate from the University of California, and specialized in equine blood typing. She was 58 years old and a widow with no children who could easily pick up and go to the four corners of the earth, and would do so to advance the study of horses. She was one of the finest professionals in her field, and gave every ounce of herself to her career and faculty.

"You know Bill, I'm sitting on the fence here. I'm not sure I should leave, but I'd like a chance to live a little before they plant me. You know since Jonas died, I haven't been anywhere or done anything but work. I'm not really sure they'd want an old bird like me."

"Ha, are you kidding? They'd jump through their turbans to get you and you know it. Why not give yourself a chance? If you think it's right and the work is good, go for it!"

"Yeah, I know. I've sent in my Curriculum Vitae, but I haven't heard anything yet. I guess it doesn't hurt to investigate it further. What about you?"

"I'm in the same boat. Guess it would depend on the work. I'd like a change of pace and scenery. Tell you the truth, though Mere, if I could team up with you again, I'd probably go."

"Now don't start that, you know how sentimental I am. But it was sure nice of you to say that. You always know how to make a girl feel good."

Meredith had met Bill seven years earlier when they both decided to continue their education, and had attended a symposium that summer. Placed together in a laboratory experiment, the two hit it off immediately and became fast friends. Meredith was drawn to Bill's constant lightheartedness and incessant humor, while Bill was impressed with Meredith's vast knowledge of technical information, accompanied by her absence of vanity and ego. She was, as he once put it, "a breath of fresh air over a stagnant pond of self-appreciation."

"No, no I mean it, Mere. If you go, I'll go."

"What about Lauren? She wouldn't let you take her away from her family and friends."

"No, it's not like that anymore," he said slowly. "We're, not, well, let's just say it doesn't matter any more. Not now."

"Well, I'm sorry to hear that Bill, I always thought you two were," she stopped short. She didn't want to lie about it, but didn't know how to finish the sentence.

"No, it's okay. We've been coasting for quite some time. I don't know what happened. I guess life just got in the way."

"Well I've gotta go, I'm late for a staff meeting. Let's think about this and get back together this week. Okay?"

"Sounds good, Mere. Hey lady, if you're in, I'm in."

"I'll call you inside a week, Bill. And thanks."

Although the tone between these old friends was professional, each valued the other's friendship almost as much as their intellectual capabilities. They not only liked one another, but in many ways needed to be in each other's lives. They were kindred spirits linked by a common bond. A bond which, in its idyllic simplicity, was a genuine love of horses. They had devoted most of their energy and time to their careers, and they knew that, in the world of medical research, you either publish or perish.

But in the twilight of the evening when they could allow their minds to settle and their souls to seep, a passion burned deep within them that forced a smile to their hearts in the sweet knowledge that for one more day, they were doing God's work. They were helping the most beautiful animals that ever graced the earth, and, in so doing, found peace of mind.

Chapter 12

1993

Jules Weherner had arrived at the Karoumi Equine Research Center just in time to meet most of the newly acquired staff at a cocktail party held in the immense and ornately decorated palace ballroom. She was formally dressed in a black sequined gown and black heels, and was in fantastic form when Prince Rajad approached her taking her hand in his. Having arrived slightly ahead of the royal party, she was on her third Old Fashioned when she felt the prince's lips on the back of her hand. She blushed, as he spoke in a low Arabian voice.

"You have made me very happy Miss Weherner, as I so hoped you would become a part of our team."

The prince, although not as experienced as his older brother in the world of social graces, had been steadily improving since his recruiting adventures began.

"Thank you, your highness," said Jules, unsure of just what to call the prince.

"Oh, please call me Rajad, and I hope we can dispense with all the formality."

"Well then, please, call me Jules," she said, pulling her shoulders tightly together, smiling seductively.

"I hope we can become friends. And in the spirit of friendship, allow me to propose a toast. To friendship."

"To friendship," echoed Jules, as their glasses clinked.

Seeing several new people to welcome, Rajad reluctantly excused himself before continuing his welcoming trek around the room. Jules, in a lather, watched the handsome prince walk away and thought, *how am I going to get my hooks into him. Or, his brother.* Seeing that Efram had arrived and had begun to greet the guests, Jules made her way over to where he was standing.

Jules Nicole Weherner, a twenty-eight year old microbiologist research assistant, was born to Simon and Golda Weherner, hard working immigrants who, as children, had barely escaped the Nazi prison camps during World War II. Simon, a nuclear physicist and a brilliant scientist in his own right, felt particularly blessed when Golda delivered their six pound, seven ounce baby girl the summer of 1967. Overindulgent with their only child they raised Jules to abhor power, deluging her with Jewish teachings and traditions while frequently drawing references to Hitler and the Holocaust, undermining her own thoughts of American values of prosperity and success.

Despite these constant overtures, they produced a prodigious young lady who, by the time she was 16, had earned a full scholarship to Emory University, graduating Magma Cum Laude with a B.S. in microbiology. Gratuitously welcomed into the graduate studies program at Cornell University, she'd developed what was to become, an unholy interest in genetics. Following two years of intense research, she was granted funding in the field of genetic typing, but a quest for furthering her own reputation instead of advancing the field of science precluded her from success.

It was due to her demonically self-serving ways, that she was asked to leave the university under questionable circumstances. Her quest for recognition and hunger for power had taken its toll. It was never disclosed publicly, nor was it placed among her transcripts, but Jules had become involved in an unethical project involving the mutation and destruction of embryonic cells, which was completely against the rules of the department. Following repeated warnings to abandon the endeavor, she was asked to withdraw from the program or face expulsion. After consulting an attorney, Jules agreed to withdraw.

Returning home to Maryland, she applied for a lab

assistant position at Montbalm Research Center. With her impeccable credentials, including her grade point average, credits earned, not to mention her pretty face and a certain look in her eye, she was hired by Dr. Bill Leach, founder of Montbalm. She was a fast tracker and Dr. Leach, seeing her enormous potential, took her under his wing. Her outstanding performance, over the next several months, earned her the trip to Karoumi as Dr. Leach's assistant.

"There you are Jules," said Dr. Leach, weaving between several guests carrying a drink in each hand. He'd been speaking with an old colleague when Jules popped into his sight. Seeing her standing alone, on the far side of the room, he felt compelled to speak to her.

"Whadda ya say we get out of here, for a while?" said Jules.

"Smoke's bothering you too, huh?"

"How'd you guess?"

"You know what they say. When in Rome, or if you can't lick 'em, join 'em."

"Yeah, but we're in Arabia and I'd rather fight than switch."

They made their way through the large arched doorway leading out to a beautifully decorated veranda of cascading fountains, hanging floral baskets and palm trees, covered with a teal green canvas awning. The late evening sky was a deep azure blue, majestically painted with the pink and orange glow of the setting sun. A quarter moon peeked above the trees, as a warm breeze kissed their faces. It was a night laden with romance and Jules was tendering the mood, as her mind gathered visions of a naked Prince Rajad.

"Boy it's good to see these folks again. Some of us go back years."

"I envy you, Bill, I really do," said Jules, as her gaze fell to the flower garden below.

"Whoa, you envy me? Why?"

"You know, you've done something with your life. I mean,

these people have such respect for you."

He felt sorry for her. In the short time she'd worked for him, they'd become close, but not as close as Jules would have liked. Although he was fond of her and had enjoyed her company over a cocktail from time to time, he'd never felt completely comfortable around her. At least not comfortable enough to allow his good judgement to be overruled by his heart or his penis. In simple terms, he was afraid of her as though her character lacked the quality necessary to resonate with his. He couldn't figure her out, not that he really wanted to, but something in his sub-conscience protected him and warned him that she was not a person with whom he could ever share a secret or a bed. Even though his was empty most of the time.

"Jules, don't give me that. I know better. There's nothing under the sun you can't do."

She didn't answer, but gazed out over the complex thinking...

Someday, I will.

Chapter 13

The Karoumi Equine Research Center (KERC) and associated training facility, known internally as the complex, was in its final stages of completion as the majority of the staff began reporting. Located approximately four miles from the edge of Beladesh on sixty acres of man-made oasis, it had been built with room to spare. The complex included the main office and reception building, a research laboratory, surgical center, race track, stables, exercise facilities and housing for the staff and visitors. It was, to say the least, state-of-the-art and world-class in every way.

It was two days following the cocktail party when Rajad sent Jules a hand written note.

> I would consider it an honor and a blessing if you would join me for dinner this evening. If this is acceptable, my car will come for you at seven.
>
> Rajad.

Surprised and elated, she scribbled the following note in reply:

> Thank you. It would be my pleasure.
>
> Jules.

"Madame, may I come for you this evening?" asked the royal servant.

"Yes, that would be fine."

"As you wish, madame," he said, bowing his head. "My

name is Sasha and I will escort you this evening."

She was pacing the living room of her spacious apartment when she heard the gentle knock on her door.

"Good evening madame."

Impressed with Darkside's humble demeanor, and warm soft voice, she couldn't help noticing his bright black eyes which sparkled with penetrating intensity, and the large birth mark on the left side of his face. Riding to the palace in the back of the royal limo, her mind was awash in thoughts of carnal pleasure.

Rajad had come to greet her as she crossed under the tall archway leading into the royal palace and, once again, kissed her hand with a loving touch. A flash of animal magnetism electrified the shallow space between them as their eyes met. Conversing during dinner, their energy seemed cosmic and their movements sensuous, as they feasted on a prepared meal of fresh gulf shrimp cocktail, marinated lamb roasted in palm leaves, steamed asparagus, a rice dish known only to the chef and a bottle of Dom Perignon vintage 1972. Following a stroll about the palace, Rajad led her to a balcony overlooking a courtyard from where they could see the evening shadows of palm trees swaying in the soft light from the torch lit pathways.

Taking her hand in his, he kissed her palm. It was not the kiss he reserved for stately greeting, but one that expressed his passion. Pulling her close and placing his lips over hers, he lingered for a moment, without pressing, allowing her body to lean into him. They kissed for a long moment as she felt herself spinning, completely suspended in time. His tongue explored the depth of her mouth as their passion escalated beyond anything she could recall. Holding her closer, she could feel the strength of his manhood pressing ever larger into her groin. Rajad slowly separated his lips from hers and gazed deep into her eyes.

"Jules, I want you."

Not wanting to give in so quickly, she had a desire to toy

with him like a cat toys with a mouse before the killing begins. Dropping her gaze she said, in a mock southern accent, "Why Rajad, I have no earthly idea what you mean."

He kissed her several times that evening, but was careful not to allow himself to go too far, because he was at the royal palace, the house of his father. He would wait for the moment to ripen, at a time and place where their passion could take center stage. A place within the walls of his own personal apartment, which Darkside maintained for him, on the outskirts of town. The evening ended with his suggestion that they meet the following afternoon to review some horses he'd purchased. Riding back to her apartment her mind was filled with thoughts of her next move and the fact that...

This is going to be some kind of adventure.

Chapter 14

Dr. Meredith Pehlagrem stood at the head of the huge mahogany table which had been set with large bowls of fruit and several cups of steaming coffee. Sporting a pale blue suit, a warm friendly face, she addressed her staff formally for the first time. Hired to direct the Karoumi Equine Research Center, soon to be known as the KERC, she'd been allowed to select, from over two hundred and fifty applications, the professionals whose careers she would direct.

"I can't believe we did it," she said, truly moved. "I'd be remiss in my spiritual and professional duties if I did not say that seeing you all together is one of the most heart-felt moments of satisfaction I have experienced in my career."

The staff members had been introduced to each other at the formal parties thrown by the prince, but this was the first time they'd been together professionally.

Speaking to her colleagues, she looked at each and every one saying, "It is my honor and privilege to be among you and I sincerely hope that together we can achieve the goals each of us has personally set."

The meeting turned into an open forum, as the members were encouraged to express their reasons for coming to Karoumi. It was apparent that most of the staff possessed a genuine desire to advance the quality of equine care. Dr. Pehlagrem promised to meet with each one individually to establish responsibilities and set personal goals. Walking back to her office following the meeting, she heard a familiar voice over her shoulder.

"So, how are things shaping up here, Mere?" asked Bill, catching up to her in the hallway.

"Pretty good all in all, but I'm not sure I want to rush

things."

She hadn't quite grasped the overall strategy and direction the royal family wanted the staff to take, but she felt extremely confident with the team she'd assembled. It appeared to her that the entire staff hungered with a passion to do something new, a mission they could complete, or a cure they could find. She'd come away from her first meeting with the feeling that the room had been alive with energy and the knowledge that each member was in the presence of a world-class affiliation.

"I think you've got the best of the best on your team, and I'm quite proud to be here."

"Thanks Bill, you're always so kind. I'm glad you're here too."

Walking to Dr. Pehlagrem's office, their conversation was business-like.

"I haven't really had much of a chance to speak to you since we got here, Bill, so tell me what you would like to do? I mean, we sort of have it made right now, so you can go in whichever direction you want, at this stage of the game."

"Yeah, I've thought about that. I've spent most of my life in the lab. I think I'd like to get out among the breed and see what's happening. Heck, I want to live a little."

"What do you have in mind?"

"I'd like to experiment with the breeding cycle. Put a few things together and see what I can come up with. The royalty wants to re-invent the Arabian breed, isn't that what I've heard?"

"That's what they say. They think it's gotten too unsound or something, but I can't say as I agree."

"I don't care what they think as long as the checks don't bounce."

"But you know, Bill, they just may have a point. Anyway, I told them we'd do the best we could."

"Mere, with the bunch you've corralled, we should be able to do just about anything."

"Just as long as we don't get too cocky. I don't know these

people, I've only hired them. They've got some mighty big plans for this place. Maybe we can get things started before our time is through."

"I'm sure we can, but until then, got any plans for dinner?"

"No, not really. Why Doctor Leach, are you asking me for a date?"

"And what if I am?"

"Then I accept."

Chapter 15

He'd wined and dined her and showed her his castle along with the stables and horses he so cherished, and it was time to take the relationship to a new level. Having sent his car for her, he instructed his driver to bring her to his private apartment. Following a glass of wine and a few moments of nervous chit chat, Rajad began kissing her softly and sweetly, until his passion grew to take on a life of its own.

With very deliberate movements, holding her eyes with his, he removed her evening gown and underclothes, stopping with each article to lick and kiss her seductively. With their nakedness on full display, he kissed the nape of her neck, chafing it with his beard causing her body to tingle and vibrate. He licked her back from side to side allowing his tongue to dawdle all the way to her buttocks.

"Ohhhhhh," she breathed, her skin turning to gooseflesh. "You are killing me. I, I can't stand it."

The more he kissed and licked, the more she moaned until she demanded. "Take me! Just take me!"

They fit together perfectly, as he penetrated her. She was hotter than she'd ever been and her head was spinning. It was the most romantic, passionate moment of her life.

Their bodies moved rhythmically to the beat of a gutsy back-alley drum, until he climaxed in a steamy crescendo, causing her to do the same. As the skyrockets lit the darkness behind her tightly closed eyes, a dam burst somewhere in her soul causing her to bite him hard on the chest as she dug her fingernails into the small of his back.

"Auggg, ohhhhhhhh. I can't. I can't," she quipped breathlessly, unaware of herself.

His ejaculation was powerful, but did not slow his pelvic motion. He remained erect and continued on for several moments until, for the first time in his life, he found himself ejaculating a second time. Covered with sweat, they lay in quiet disbelief of their collective experience.

"Are you for real?" Jules asked, finally. "I mean, I've never, I mean, you, you are the best. The best!"

"We, are the best," whispered Rajad. "We are the very best."

The days passed seductively with Rajad and Jules acting like two kids in a candy store, their lovemaking growing more frenzied each time they'd meet. Reaching a magic level of comfort and trust, they'd begun to disclose their inner-most secrets, as the elixir of infatuation fooled their hearts into thinking they were falling in love. It was on one such occasion that Rajad told Jules of his dream to develop a new breed of racehorse. One for which Karoumi and the KERC would be forever known.

"Can you see them? Prancing about the stables. I want so much for the people of Karoumi, to be proud. Proud of their heritage."

"I can understand that," said Jules. "I've always been proud to be an American."

"Americans have so very much for which to be proud, but we in Karoumi do not. Not until now."

"So what's so different about now?"

"The research center. You. All the people who will be helping me create the master breed." Rajad's eyes sparkling, as he spoke.

"The master breed?"

"The master breed. The new Thoroughbred. The new Arabian. I am not quite sure. Tell me my dear, how much do you know about cloning?"

"Cloning? I thought you said a new breed?"

"I want the best breed."

"I don't know. I don't think you can clone a horse. I'm not sure it's even legal."

"In Karoumi, if I say it is legal, it is legal."

Although stunned with his response, Jules, nonetheless

liked what she'd heard.

He makes the rules here. Not the police. Not government. Not God. Not anyone, but him. Wow!

"Cloning? Hmm, I'm not sure I'd even know where to begin."

Her mind was already thinking about the details, even though she was pretty sure it was impossible.

"That is where you come in. I know nothing of this process, but you, you are an expert."

"I'm no expert. I mean I understand the basic concepts, but cloning a horse?"

"Now imagine if we could clone two of the most famous horses of all time. Could we not then generate a master breed?"

"Well, in theory, anything's possible, but here? I mean how could you do it? I mean, you know, without everyone knowing?"

They bantered lightheartedly for several minutes, until it was time for her to leave, but her curiosity was piqued as thoughts of the cloning process filled her mind.

Where would you start? What horse would you choose? How much DNA would you need?

Chapter 16

It was to Jules' benefit that Dr. Pehlagrem had assigned her the task of overseeing the development of the equine library, located on the second floor of the complex. She was to order, at her own discretion, the necessary books, magazines, periodicals and research papers, the doctors and scientists would need to remain abreast of the industry, while enjoying a seemingly unlimited budget with which to work. With her curiosity piqued, she began reading everything she could find about cloning. The more she researched, the more dissatisfied she became with the lack of progress in the field.

In her research, she'd stumbled across several articles pertaining to the lineage of horses, particularly the famous and extremely successful Thoroughbreds. Having worked in the equine industry for only a short period of time, she was unaware that racehorses have two separate careers, one as a racing competitor, where they usually earn their name and fame, and, upon retirement from the track, a second career as a sire or dam. Some are good on the track while others are good in the breeding shed, but achieving the pinnacle of success in both arenas is rare.

Horses like Nearco who sired several big stakes winners, among them, Nashrulla, sire of Nashua, the first Thoroughbred to sell for over a million dollars. And Bold Ruler, stallion of the year seven consecutive times, producing a gargantuan number of famous horses, not the least of which was Secretariat. But none had ever been so important to Thoroughbred racing as Northern Dancer, winner of the 1964 Kentucky Derby and Preakness. When Norther Dancer entered stud during the fall of 1964, the world record price for a Thoroughbred yearling had reached $170,000. Less than twenty years later, one of his sons sold for over ten million dollars, while one of his grandsons brought over thirteen million. Between 1966 and 1988, Northern Dancer's 295 yearlings sold for a grand total 184 million dollars, averaging $620,000 apiece. Northern Dancer himself had changed the face of modern Thoroughbred racing, as greater than half of all the world's Thoroughbred racehorses would claim his blood in their pedigree.

Jules began to understand just how important so very few of these great animals were to the overall lineage. And that if only a handful were taken out of the picture, the Thoroughbred breeding industry would be significantly altered. It might even collapse.

What if just the right horses were to be removed; rendered incapable of building a progeny? she wondered. *How would this affect the Thoroughbred industry today? What if, instead of cloning a master breed, one could control the industry? Could a substance be developed and administered to an animal in such a way as to mask its delivery and residence, while secretly destroying the offspring? A substance which could affect DNA.*

She knew it could, and was on the verge of proving it, when she was asked to leave Cornell University. Always a fan of the effects of testosterone, she would inject herself with the male hormone to maintain a more potent sex drive, allowing her to achieve deeper and more frequent orgasms. Failing to detect changes in her mood which caused her to become more aggressive, her fascination didn't stop with merely using the synthetic hormone. She began a series of questionable experiments that placed her in a precarious position among her classmates and instructors.

It's hard to say what makes one person good and another one evil, whether it's genetics, karma, or the way of God. Jules had come from good parents and had been given every opportunity to develop herself along ethical lines, but it always seemed that whenever confronted with a choice, she chose the wicked path. Unconscionable, self-serving and, in a morbid way, destructively controlling, she would have been an all-American candidate at torture, if the sports world incorporated torture in its wide world of endeavor.

Her theory was that a genetic substance could lie dormant in the molecules of body cells, activating in the male testes with the explosive power of testosterone during the manufacture of semen. And, when passed to the egg during fertilization, could alter the DNA code, affecting the offspring. She wasn't completely sure of the altering capabilities, but she knew a variety of results were possible. She was fully aware that she wasn't getting any younger, and that now was the time to finally perfect her theory and put it to the test.

It was this way of thinking and her reputation, both in and out of the classroom, that caused enough concern with the ethics committee who recommended that she be dismissed from the college of Veterinary Medicine in Ithaca, New York.

Chapter 17

It was during one of their steamy interludes, that Jules told Rajad about her darkened past. With her clear understanding of several interesting related subjects, linking topics such as equine medicine, horse husbandry, clinical pathology and the afterglow of awesome sex, it wasn't difficult for her to persuade Rajad not to attempt to clone a master breed, but to alter the current ones. Lying naked on the huge circular bed puffing a Turkish cigarette, he finally broke his pensive silence with a childlike question.

"Is it truly possible to do this?"

"I believe I can. I do believe I can."

It was her ticket to stardom and she knew it. If she could pull it off, she could control her destiny both as a scientist and possibly as the wife of a wealthy Arabian prince. Her time was now, and her future lay before her cloaked in evil selfishness and genetic hell.

"I mean, I believe it will do what you want it to do, but I can't be sure, you know, not completely sure."

She wanted to remain in his good graces in the event the project was a failure.

"What is it you think I want it to do?"

"Control."

"Control? Control what?"

"Do you know what the most powerful force in nature is?" she asked, coyly.

"My own ego?"

"Close. Sorry, my dear, but it's the male sex drive."

"The male sex drive? You mean like mine?" Rajad was pumping his pelvis as he laughed.

"You might think it's funny, but it's true. Do you have any

idea just how powerful testosterone is? It's the engine of life."

Standing over the bed continuing to talk, she took his flaccid penis between her thumb and index finger.

"One tiny droplet of sperm from this little guy can procreate an entire species. When you play with testosterone, there's no telling what can happen. It's like dynamite."

"So what does this mean? You can develop a genetic dynamite?"

Looking deep into his eyes, she began to take on a devilish attitude, placing her knee on the bed, while turning her head slowly towards the wall catching her reflection in the mirror. Noticing how sexy she looked, she started to primp, allowing her eyes to find his.

"I can become God."

Rajad had never seen her like this and didn't know if he liked it.

"I can develop a substance that can change the reproductive process. I can destroy."

"Wait, wait a minute. What do you mean, you can become God? No one can become God."

Realizing she might have gone too far, she began explaining.

"Have you ever heard of a drug called Thalidomide?"

"Of course not. What do I know about drugs?"

"Thalidomide was given to pregnant women back in the sixties, which caused all kinds of birth defects. Babies with no fingers, some with no hands and even no arms or legs. What I'm proposing is something like that."

"I don't want to do anything like that," said Rajad, his black eyes flashing.

"I want to produce a pure breed of animal, not destroy one."

"Think about it. I can develop a drug that will allow you to do whatever you want."

"And how will this do that for me?"

"It will allow you to take control. Take full control," she

hissed slowly, her eyes half closed.

"You mean I could control the horses of the world with this drug?"

She didn't answer, but allowed the thought to sink in. Her mind drifted back to Cornell and the experiments she'd conducted before being asked to leave. She knew that if Rajad went along with her evil scheme, that she would need complete privacy. If the prince opened the necessary doors, she felt she could succeed.

"What you are talking about is not good," he said.

"No, no, you're missing the point. You want to start a newer, better breed, right? Think of it this way. Someday you might, if you're lucky, clone a fabulous horse like Man-o-War. Then you could breed the best mares to him, or clone a filly like Ruffian and breed her to him. But, you're looking at years to complete that process. What I'm talking about is right now."

"I do not see what you mean."

"If we could cause a major problem in the Thoroughbred or the Arabian horse industry, and bring about a debilitating disease, then we could bring about the cure. I mean right here in Karoumi. You would have the whole world coming to you both for the cure and, eventually, to produce the new breed. You would have the best of all worlds."

The last statements Jules made registered heavily in Rajad's mind. This was exactly what he'd wanted when he convinced his father to accept the idea of a world-class research center. It was unfortunate that he had no idea he was succumbing to the control of a wickedly dangerous lady. Fully aware that she knew nothing about a cure for the malady she was advocating, Jules didn't care. Her only interest was in gaining control of a wealthy prince who could facilitate her fanciful dreams and provide the wealth and power for which she so hungered.

"Do you really think you can make this thing?"

"Yeah, I do. But, I'll need your help."

"My help, what do I know of such things?"

"Not your knowledge, honey, just your help getting me the things I'll need. I know I'll need a lab of my own and some privacy. But I still don't know what to do about Doctor Pehlagrem."

"What about Doctor Pehlagrem?"

"Well we certainly can't take a chance on her finding out, and she's kinda like a mother hen. I mean she's in everybody's business."

"Well, she is the director, that is what she is supposed to do."

"I know, I know and she does a wonderful job, almost too good. Well anyway, you'll have to find a way to get her off my back."

Rajad wasn't completely sure what this substance could do for him, or whether he should allow it to be developed, but thoughts of controlling the industry were exciting. Not to be overshadowed by the fact that what he wanted most of all, for once in his life, was to be more successful than his older and more dominant brother. It was very exciting... the most exciting thing he'd felt in a long, long time.

Chapter 18

For the next several days, Jules went about her work in the library until one afternoon when she was summoned to Dr. Pehlagrem's office.

"Jules, come in and make yourself comfortable. Tell me, how do you like Karoumi?"

"I really like it. I mean it's a little hotter than what I'm used to, but it agrees with me."

"You must have really impressed the royal family, they have asked me if you could have exclusive use of the lower lab for awhile."

"Oh yes, I asked if I could use that on my own time, since it's not completely finished yet. I mean, I hope I didn't overstep my boundaries, Doctor?"

"It's Meredith, and no, not at all. I think it's a wonderful idea. I always appreciate initiative. Can you tell me what it is you're doing, or is it a secret?"

"No ma'am, it's not a secret. I want a place to meditate and allow my mind to flow freely. It's not so much a project as just a place to become more in tune with my inner conscience. I always work better that way."

Jules was a master at masking the truth. Even though she was lying to Meredith, she did feel a need to be alone with her work, and so felt justified in stretching the truth.

"Jules, I like the way you think."

"I just thought that if no one had plans for that space and since it's not completely finished, I might use it. Of course, with your permission."

"I envy you, Jules. And from what I've heard about you from Doctor Leach, you are one smart cookie. He certainly has big plans for you."

"Thank you Doctor. Coming from you, that's quite a compliment. He certainly speaks highly of you, I know that."

"Oh?" asked Meredith, inquisitively.

"When he found out that you had decided to take this job, he wasn't the same person. He was a changed man. Like he usually gets around Christmas. You know, cheerful all the time, not always serious and businesslike."

"Oh, that's just the way he is. You can't pay any attention to that. I love working with that old rascal."

They talked for several minutes, mostly about the abstract elements of research, until Meredith asked Jules if she needed her assistance with anything. Not believing she was able to pull it off so smoothly, Jules thanked Meredith profusely, as she exited her office. Feeling like she was suspended from the sky, she returned to the library, where she plotted to begin her unholy work as soon as the staff left for the day.

Although the lab in the basement wasn't completely finished, Jules, with the help of Rajad, managed to procure most everything she'd asked for within a few weeks, including a bathroom and two separate water supplied sinks. A refrigeration unit, a centrifuge, several Bunsen burners along with the various glass flasks and tubes she would need. Tables, bookshelves, microscopes, lighting fixtures, a bed for napping and, last but not least, a lock on the door.

The next several weeks found her working late into the night accompanied from time to time by Rajad. When they weren't alone in the lab, they were alone in his apartment, where their love affair was continually reaching newer and higher vistas.

"Why not come to live in the apartment?" he asked one night.

"Are you serious? What would people say?"

"Who cares, I make the rules here."

"Would you live there too?"

"You know I cannot do that. But I could be there often." Rajad's black eyes had a way of penetrating her. He was extremely charming when he wanted to be, and could turn it on at will.

"Let me think about it. I mean, I just don't know."

He took both her hands in his and kissed them softly saying, "My dear, it would make me very happy."

Sensing an uncontrollable need within the prince, Jules saw something flash from within his eyes, feeling for a fleeting moment that she was in harm's way. Allowing his grip to tighten around her wrist, making her uncomfortable, he said. "I need you. Now!"

"I'll think about it," she whispered, as he slowly released her, holding her rigidly within his gaze.

Chapter 19

Months later

The alabaster desk gleamed pearl white and gray, as the light from the large oval skylight fell softly over the center of the sheikh's inner office. Four calf skin leather chairs formed a semi circle about the sheikh's desk, while several over-stuffed hand-stitched couches in the regal colors of burgundy and cream stripes with a tinge of mint green, rimmed the outer walls. The decor was austere by most Arabian standards, but when the light shone just right through the skylight, it presented a heavenly glow and bathed the inner sanctum in celestial warmth. The sheikh paced around his desk looking at Efram while the two of them waited for Rajad to join them.

"You must not confront your brother directly with this. He will be defensive, especially if he feels you are involved," said the sheikh to Efram regarding Rajad's budgetary mismanagement.

"I should probably discuss this with him alone."

"As you wish, Father," said Efram preparing to leave, but as he rose from his chair, Rajad knocked and entered the inner office. Seeing his brother and father together always placed him in a defensive posture.

"Rajad, come in my son, Efram was just leaving. How are things at the Training Center?"

Rajad, looking first at Efram and then at his father answered, "We have had some minor problems, but nothing serious."

"I must go," said Efram moving toward the door. "I am late for a meeting, so until later." He bowed and closed the door behind him.

The sheikh, never a man to waste time nor words said,

"Rajad, it is unfortunate that I must confront you today about your budget. Please, sit down."

Rajad knew immediately that Efram had been to the sheikh complaining about his lavish spending, but he didn't think he was that far outside the boundary of good management.

"Father, I can explain, we have had some unexpected costs, but..."

"Rajad, please, this is not a trifling matter. You know how the council works. You have been given everything you have asked for, and now it is time you found a way to remain in compliance with the rest of us. I, as well as my constituents, believe you have performed brilliantly, and we all are very proud of you. But you must be patient with your spending and remain within your budget."

"Did Efram have anything to do with this?"

"If he did, what difference would it make? Would you rather someone outside our family bring this to my attention? He has brought this to me to save you the embarrassment."

"HE is my embarrassment."

"He is your brother, you must never forget that. He will be there for you when everyone else has rejected you. He is your blood."

The tension in the room was beginning to tighten, as the sheikh's face grew red. Rajad had not noticed this in his father before, but sensed that it was not a good time to argue.

"Father, I am sorry, I guess I owe him an apology. I am happy that he has come forward with this, I just wish he would have thought to talk to me first."

"I understand that, my son. You are correct. Maybe if you would speak to him, he will feel compelled in the future to come to you first. You know, Rajad, my only wish is for the two of you to work together in harmony. For the two of you to live long and joyously after I am gone. That is my only desire."

But, as Rajad left his father's office, a different drum was beating within his savage heart. He went immediately to confront Efram and would have had it not been for a call that he'd received inside his royal limousine.

"Hey, lover."

"Jules, I am in no mood."

"What's wrong?"

"Please, do not bother me now. I am very angry."

"Well, I've got something that just might cheer you up. A little bottle of nose spray. Why not stop by the lab?"

"You mean?" Rajad's mood was about to change.

Over the next several weeks Rajad toyed with ideas of implementing a plan to infect a select group of Kentucky Thoroughbred racehorses with the genetic substance Jules had developed. If this genetic substance could do what he and Jules thought it could, it was the beginning of the end and just a matter of time before the racing world would come to him. A world reborn in Karoumi.

It was a fantastic idea. And who could he rely upon to deliver such a plan? Who had the brains, savvy and infiltration skills to carry out such an evil deed? But, most importantly, who was loyal enough to be trusted? Someone with style, class and just the right attitude. Someone who owed his life to him. Someone with a birthmark on his face.

Chapter 20

The evening sky was almost dark and the stars were just beginning to appear, as Darkside drove Rajad in the black Mercedes sedan on a lonely stretch of road out into the desert.

"I am your loyal servant, my Prince."

"When you return from Istanbul," said Rajad. "I will need you to deliver a package for me. A very special package. One that will take you to America and to the state of Kentucky to stay for a few weeks. Only you and I are to know of this plan. We are the only ones who will ever know. You must leave no trace, but you must find an individual to assist you in your task."

"My Prince, your every request is my command."

"This will place Karoumi on the map and bring the riches of the world lapping at our feet like dogs, my loyal friend. I would not trust this plan to anyone but you."

The limousine moved slowly along the newly paved road silhouetted against the blue-black evening sky, while Rajad conveyed his plan of lethal extermination from the back seat of the car.

Late that night, Darkside and two of his compatriots flew to Istanbul to visit an old adversary and settle an old debt. As Nazr the Nazi emerged from his nightly duties the three men, waiting outside the prison, followed him, cornering him in a dark alley a few blocks from where Darkside had been incarcerated. The men surrounded the hateful prison guard, as Nazr, realizing he'd been captured, fell to his knees pleading for his life.

"Stand up, you gutless pig!" ordered Darkside.

"Please, please, I was under orders. You must believe me."

"Of course you were. Just as I am. I am ordering myself to

kill you."

They forced a rag into Nazr's mouth and handcuffed his hands behind his back, as one of the men produced a small acetylene torch and a long metal rod from the trunk of the car. Lighting the torch, he held the flame against the end of the rod until it glowed red hot. With the men each kneeling on one of Nazr's shoulders, pinning him to the ground, Darkside stood over the heavy-set guard holding the metal rod.

"Do you remember all the times you tortured me? Asked Darkside, slowly pressing the red-hot metal branding iron into Nazr's forehead. Holding it in place for over five seconds, the sickening smell of burning flesh invaded their nostrils, as Nazr shook violently trying to free himself from the hellish ordeal. With a small flashlight they could see the brand they had made on the prison guard's forehead. A symbol befitting his terrible nature. A symbol of one of the most vile and hateful times in human history. The symbol of Hitler's Third Reich, a swastika.

"Do you remember how many times you raped me? Do you remember all the prisoners you raped and killed? No? Well, maybe this will help you."

Unsheathing a six inch knife from the back of his belt, one of the men quickly cut away the guard's pants. With Nazr squirming in pain, the other man grabbed Nazr's shrunken penis and pulled it out, exposing it for all to see.

"You will not be raping anyone else. I can assure you of that," said Darkside. Running the knife along Nazr's penis for several moments, Darkside gazed at the shear terror in the prison guard's eyes, and realized he could not bring himself to finish the barbarous task.

"Leave him," said Darkside. "He will carry that brand for the rest of his life. Live with that you disgusting pig, you are not worth killing."

Chapter 21

Lexington, Kentucky - 1995

Smoke plumes drifted upwardly towards the garish chrome plated ceiling of the dimly lit barroom just off Main Street in downtown Lexington. A statue of a smiling, naked woman with enormous breasts stood center stage of the oval shaped bar, as jazz sounds wafted from speakers impregnating the red velvet covered walls.

Perched on his black leather stool, Jefferson Fairchild sat sipping a gin and tonic when he noticed a dark, handsome man making his way toward the opposite side of the bar. Jimmy Devil's was known throughout the city as a wild and sometimes weird place catering to Lexington's large and ever-growing theater community.

Known by his friends as Jeff, the middle-aged farmer cast a delectably smug appearance as he sat sipping his drink with his mind attuned to either his next dollar or sexual encounter, whichever came first. His best quality was the way Mother Nature had blessed him with a tall, slim 6' 2" frame upon which he carried 225 pounds of solid muscle. He had curly blond hair, light brown eyes and somewhat of a Robert Redford look about him. Lettering in four sports in high school and quarterbacking the Cobb County Cougers to their first Class AA Football State Championship, he'd developed a cavalier attitude and Hollywood demeanor. Not a slave to fashion, he usually wore standard horseman's garb of khaki pants, long sleeve button down oxford shirt and brown desert boots. Most of those who knew him liked him, but due to an over abundance of self-esteem and insensitivity, he did have his enemies.

Sipping his drink, he noticed a man on the other side of the bar whom he'd seen around every night for the last couple of days. Preparing to launch his best pickup line on a tall brunette sitting at a table behind him, his thoughts were interrupted when the bartender brought him a fresh drink saying, "From the guy over there," nodding in the stranger's direction. "The one with that big mark on his face."

How'd he know me, thought Jeff, as he thanked the bartender while nodding to the stranger.

Glancing over at Jeff, the stranger lifted his glass as if to propose a toast. Jeff, intrigued, slid off the stool lifting his glass in response.

Walking over to his newly found friend, he said, "Do I know you?"

"My name is Sasha and I am here on business."

"Jeff Fairchild, good to meetcha."

"I am told that you are the man to see about horses."

"Oh really? You looking for anything special?"

"I am looking for special horses."

"Well now, you've come to the right place. This here's the horse capital of the world and I'm the horseman of the county."

Darkside had done his homework. He knew Jeff was heavily in debt and on the verge of losing his farm. A farm he'd inherited that had been in his family for several generations.

"Allow me to explain myself," said Darkside. "I am in search of someone who can help me understand the horse business."

"Oh yeah? Whaddya need to know?"

After several drinks, Darkside knew that he'd made the right choice. He'd found his flunky - his access to the horses.

Chapter 22

It was nearing noon when they'd decided to meet the next morning for breakfast to discuss their business. They sat drinking hot coffee at the local Cracker Barrel restaurant, as Jeff listened to what Darkside had to say.

"I am prepared to pay you $10,000 dollars now and an additional $50,000 if my mission is successful."

Jeff's eyes widened, as he stopped chewing his mouthful of biscuits and gravy. He wasn't sure he'd heard the man correctly, his mind jumping to calculate how quickly he could pay off the newly acquired mortgage on his farm. Gulping his food, he took a large drink of steaming coffee, burning his mouth. Flinching, but hardly noticing the pain, he said...

"Now let me get this straight. You want me to show you some of the horse farms around here? And for that you'll pay me $60,000 dollars?"

His astonishment at the large sum, overcame his uneasiness about the deal.

"That is correct."

"Why me?" he asked, shrugging his shoulders. He knew he might have a reputation as a cad and a drunk with a gambling addiction, but Jefferson Fairchild was nobody's fool.

"I will need your assistance in one other matter, but I am not prepared to discuss it here. With your permission, we can discuss it after we eat. Maybe you can show me the fabulous Bluegrass and we can talk in the privacy of your car."

Holding his fork three inches from his mouth, showing off his large diamond horseshoe ring, Jeff's eyes shifted left to right. His curiosity, at an all time high following Darkside's proposal, rendered him speechless. Gulping his coffee, he flagged down the waitress.

Pulling out of the parking lot, Jeff felt uneasy about the amount of much money he would earn for so little work, but instructed Darkside to drive to Calumet Farm. The bright sun burned off the fleeting remnants of mid-morning fog, as he probed Darkside for more information.

"So, what do I hafta do to earn all this money?"

"It depends on the stallions."

"Stallions?" Jeff's mind lurched into high gear. "What stallions?"

"You must tell me which of the stallions in Kentucky are the most valuable."

"Are you looking to breed?"

"It is possible, but I will not be making that decision. I am only a representative of a very wealthy man."

Beginning to relax, Jeff began piecing it all together. This guy was an Arab and he was working for one of those oil barrens he'd heard about. *Boy oh boy oh boy*, he thought, *my ship has just come in.*

"Well, I don't know, I'll have to look into it. Might take awhile. Normally I know three or four, but I don't know them all. Anyway, what happens after I find out?"

"I will need to know the ten best stallions in Kentucky. The absolute best of the best."

"And that's all, that's all I have to do to earn $60,000 dollars is to give you a list of the top ten stallions in Kentucky?"

"There will be one additional matter. And if you can do this, you will have $60,000 dollars. I will give you $10,000 when you have the list."

"And the rest? I mean the other 50?"

"You will be fully paid when the mission is complete."

As the car pulled into Calumet Farm Darkside was moved by the sheer beauty of the countryside. It was early April and the fields were lush and green nestled against the picturesque serenity of the endless white fences surrounding the immaculate farm.

Calumet Farm, located about six miles from downtown Lexington, was inherited in 1931 by Warren Wright Sr. and immediately converted from a Standardbred farm to a Thoroughbred breeding and racing establishment. With the purchase of two stallions in 1936 named Bull Lea and Blenheim II, Calumet began its dominant reign which would last through three decades.

Blenheim II sired the fabulous Whirlaway, winner of the 1941 Triple Crown. But Calumet's success was due to the offspring produced by Bull Lea who led the General Sire List in 1952 and '53 and the Broodmare Sire List in 1958, '59, '60 and '61. Among his progeny were Bewitch, Coaltown, Hill Gail, winner of the 1952 Kentucky Derby, and Iron Liege, Kentucky Derby winner in 1957. But many argue that his most famous son, Citation, the 1948 Triple Crown winner, was the best racehorse in American history. The standing debate among horseman, especially whenever a horse is on the verge of winning the Triple Crown, is who among Man O' War, Citation and Secretariat was the greatest of all time. But no one disputes that, in its day, Calumet Farm was the number one horse farm.

Walking around the horse graveyard on the backside of the farm, Jeff began telling Darkside about Alydar whose grand dam, Two Lea was the daughter of Bull Lea.

"There was a big stink about the death of Alydar here at Calumet. Remember, Alydar was the runner-up to Affirmed in the Triple Crown races. Those two raced several times, but Alydar came in second to him in all three races. Rumor had it the farm owner broke his leg just to collect the insurance money. Not many people know what really happened, but I know. Don't like to admit it, but I do."

"How much money did they collect?"

"As I recall, it was well over 35 million."

"Was he worth that much?"

"In my opinion he was priceless. Hell, they'd breed him about 200 times a year. And he'd bring two hundred grand each time. If he'd lived to be 25 years old, go figure. But he was more than that. He and Affirmed ran the greatest Triple Crown I ever saw."

"When was that?"

"That was, let's see, yeah, that was in '78. Alydar is the only horse to run second in all three races and Affirmed is the last one to win the Triple Crown. They ran together like they had the same heartbeat. Never saw anything like it. After this, I'll take you over to see Affirmed. He's still standing not far from here."

"What is this Triple Crown?"

"You don't know about the big three? It's horse racing's greatest achievement. It's made up of three races beginning in the spring. There's the Derby, I mean the Kentucky Derby in Louisville. That's the first one and it's run the first Saturday in May. Most of the stakes races during the first four months of the year are considered Derby prep races. The hardest thing about the Derby is that it's a mile and a quarter. Hell most three-year olds haven't ever run that far and most can't that early."

"Why do they push the horses so far so early?"

"That's a good question. Some trainers won't go near the Derby. Say it's just too far too soon. Hell a good horse might get lucky in the Derby and then fold after that. It takes a warrior to run well in all three races, much less win."

"What are the other races?"

"Well, second there's the Preakness, run in Maryland two weeks after the Derby. Now that's only a mile and three sixteenths. Never could figure why the Derby is longer than the Preakness, but that's just the way it is, but the turns on that track are much harder to negotiate. And then there's the Belmont run in New York three weeks after the Preakness. Now that's a real heart breaker there. That thing is a mile and a half long."

They drove around the Bluegrass visiting half a dozen horse farms, including Jonabel Farm where Affirmed stood.

Jeff seemed to know his stuff, when it came to which horse won which race and the approximate value of each. Darkside was impressed, but he was buying time searching for the perfect opportunity to tell Jeff exactly what he had to do to earn his money.

"Tell ya what," said Jeff. "I know about this party next weekend. If you ain't doing anything, why not come along. I guarantee you ain't never been to a party like this."

"I will be in town until my business is complete. When will you have the list?" asked Darkside, ignoring the invitation to the party.

"I need a couple of days. I have to make some phone calls. You know, it's not as easy as it looks."

"Take what time you will need. I am in no hurry. I must know the ten best stallions in Kentucky. You must be discreet, however."

"I'll tell you what. I'll get the ten highest paid fee studs I can find. I know of three or four and I know, let's see, I know you'll want Prince of Dreams and probably Flight Whisper, those are two of the best. That I do know. I'll have a list together by next weekend. Before the party I told you about. Whadda ya think?"

Darkside did not answer, but gazed out the window, as the car proceeded on its trek around the Bluegrass.

Chapter 23

It took Jeff several days to procure the top ten stallion list in Central Kentucky. Sitting in Jeff's truck, Darkside began his explanation as to what Jeff had to do to earn the remainder of his money.

"I have in my possession a vial of containing a very specific drug. It is a nose spray. You must get close enough to each horse and spray it directly into the horse's nostrils. You must ensure that each horse's nostrils are adequately sprayed. That is what you must do to earn the rest of the money."

"Nose spray? What kind of nose spray?"

"That is no concern of yours."

"Now wait a minute, is this some kind of poison?" Jeff's instincts were alerted; something was wrong and he didn't like it.

"Not at all. Let us say that it will have no affect on the horses."

"Then what's it for?"

"That is no concern of yours."

Jeff was caught. He surely didn't want to damage any racehorses, but he needed the money.

"What will this nose spray do?"

"I am not at liberty to discuss that with you. If you want the job, it is yours. If you do not, I will find someone else."

"No, no I'm in. I just want to know if it will hurt the horses."

"I can promise you that it will not hurt the horses."

Jeff didn't like it at all. He knew he wouldn't nor couldn't bring himself to damage one of his own. One of Kentucky's own. Not him. Not what was almost his own flesh and blood. He was confused and his mind was in turmoil.

"Are you sure it won't hurt, in any way? It won't cause any damage? I mean won't hurt them at all?"

"I am sure that nothing will happen to the horses."

"Will it change them? I mean, what is this stuff?"

"They will feel no pain and they will feel no different," said Darkside, impatiently.

"Why? I mean, why?"

"That is not for you to know. If you do not want to do this, I will understand. I will find someone else."

"Okay, okay. I'll do it, but, you won't tell anyone, will you? I mean will anyone know about this beside us?"

"No one will ever know of your involvement. Only me. I will leave here when the mission is complete and no one will ever know."

"Okay, I'm in."

Chapter 24

If Jeff was a stand in for Robert Redford, Franke 'Boy' Wilson was a dead ringer for Major Frank Burns, the bumbling character made famous in the MASH television series, only smaller, dumber and dirtier. Franke, nothing more than a stumble-bum, was a sad story, having run away from his grandmother's home the summer of his fifteenth year, after receiving a failing report card and knowing that he would again have to repeat the sixth grade. Although his grandmother tried and was good to Franke, she was hardly a successful parent, or the role model he so desperately needed. Old and in feeble health, she cared for the boy after his own mother disappeared when he was only three-years old, which damaged him psychologically leaving the toddler with a bad stutter.

Jefferson Davis Fairchild, the sole offspring of Myron and Leena Fairchild, whose family trees both contained members who'd fought in the Civil War, convinced his parents that they should allow Franke to live in the barn out behind the main house. In poor health and with no reasonable means of support, Franke accepted their kind offer, and moved into the tack room in the back of the barn. When Jeff's parents passed away, Franke became his whole family. Now Franke was about to receive the only fortunate break his miserable life would ever know.

"I need you to do something. And you can't mess this up, hear?" said Jeff, as he cornered Franke in one of the horse stalls.

Franke, not very attentive after a night of cheap wine said. "S, So, what else is na, new."

"Look, this is a chance of a lifetime, you can earn some real bread. You with me?"

"What da, do, ya wa, want?"

"I need you to spray some stuff in some horses noses."

"What? Yer k, k, kiddin' me," laughed Franke.

"Look, I'm gonna drive you to a farm. At night. You're gonna sneak in the barn. And yer gonna spray some stuff up a horse's nose. Think you can do that, asshole?"

Franke just shrugged his shoulders.

"I'll pay you $500.00 dollars for every horse."

"Five hund." Franke had never seen $500.00 dollars in his life. He'd never had $100.00 dollars at one time in his life.

"Yup, $500.00 dollars per horse."

"Shiiiiiiiit, what da, do I ha, have to da, do?"

"Not only that, I'm gonna drive you to ten farms. That's $500.00 dollars times ten. You know how much that is?"

"Uh, na, no."

"That's $5,000.00 dollars, Franke. $5,000.00 DOLLARS boy."

Franke went numb, looking at Jeff with a vacant stare.

"You mean, I'm gon, gonna ga, get five th, thousand dollars?" Franke whispered while continuing to stare.

"You got it."

Jeff was easing up. He knew how to handle Franke, but he didn't know how Franke'd handle the thought of so much money.

"You and me boy, you and me. And don't worry, I'm gonna be there with you. I'll have the binoculars on you the whole time."

The rusty old Studebaker truck crept along Toms Mill Pike about 14 miles from Lexington and pulled off the narrow two lane road behind a stand of dense pine trees. The driver, wearing all black clothes with a black hood pulled tight around his head, looked through a pair of Army field glasses, watching his villainous cohort sneak up behind the stallion barn at Turbalinda Farm.

Sneaking into the barn, Franke entered the stall of one of the most prolific breeding studs in modern times. Since the intruder had been working around horses all day, he possessed a friendly smell about him and Royal Thunder, thinking he was about to be either fed or groomed, did not act nervous at the foreigner's presence.

Producing a small silver bottle from his jacket, a large portion of a foreign substance was sprayed into the right nostril of the multi-million dollar animal. Royal Thunder jerked away, but did not make a sound, as Franke fed the horse a cube of sugar before spraying a second blast into his left nostril. Scratching the big horse on his chin, Franke slipped slowly out of the stall to proceed to his next illicit rendezvous and the eminent destruction of God's most beautiful creature. Clicking shut the stall door, and turning to move out of the barn, Franke heard...

"Franke, izzatchew? Well, I'll be hot danged. I ain't seen you in a coon's age, boy. What in blazes are you doing here?" asked Ruben Johnson, a groom with Turbalinda Farm, startling Franke.

Stumbling for words, Franke said, "Nothin', I mean I was ju, just lo, lookin' around."

"You looking for work, you come to the right place. Hell man, weun's busy 'round here. They's payin' six a hour and some of us gits more'n that. Why not ask the boss man if he'd put ya on?"

"O, O Okay, I wa, wa, will," said Franke looking around to see if anyone else had come in the barn.

"You want me to ask him for ya?"

"Na, na, no, I kin da, do it m, m, myself. Wa, where's he a, a, at?"

"He's probably over at the foaling barn. You know where that's at?"

"Yeah, wa, well I ga, guess I ga, gotta be ga, goin."

"Well don't git any lipstick on yer dipstick, dude," said Ruben laughing.

Franke hurried out the back of the barn and, as soon as he cleared the door, broke into a dead run across the field from which he'd come. He wasn't sure if he should tell Jeff that he'd been seen, but he couldn't really worry about that now, as they had other farms to visit and he had more money to make.

"Ja do it?" asked Jeff.

"Ya, yup. No pr, pr, problem."

"Anybody see ya?"

"Na, na, no man."

"What the heck you runnin so fast for? Boy, you look like you seen a ghost."

"Ja, just in a hurry. Tha, that's all."

"In a hurry to make that money huh?" laughed Jeff.

It took them three nights to complete their evil mission, visiting three farms the first and second nights and the final four on the third night. Jeff, confident he'd pulled it off, called Darkside, informing him of his success only to find he'd vacated his hotel room.

"So, where ya been? I was afraid you'd left town," said Jeff the following evening, when he saw Darkside sitting on the far side of the bar in exactly the same place where they'd first met.

"How are things?"

"Finished."

"Then let us go for a ride."

They drove around the outskirts of Lexington where Jeff informed Darkside of his previous night's adventures, including the names and whereabouts of the farms and the horses he'd infected.

"Did anyone see you?"

"No one. No one knows about this except me and you."

Carrying a concealed 9mm Smith and Wesson under his jacket, Darkside listened carefully to each and every detail. But, as he continued to drive, he knew that he could not bring himself to complete his mission. The mission he'd sworn to his prince he'd finish, several weeks earlier. It wasn't that he couldn't take another person's life, that wasn't it at all. How many times in prison had he dreamt of strangling Nazr the Nazi with his bare hands and how many nights had thoughts of the fat, disgusting guard choking to death, pleading for his life, kept him sane through the long and torturous ordeal. No, it was the fact that he was not without heart. And now he realized again, just like with Nazr, that he was no killer. He just couldn't bring himself to shoot Jefferson Fairchild.

"You have done well, my friend," said Darkside handing Jeff an envelope.

"You have earned this money."

It was the easiest money Jefferson Fairchild ever earned.

Chapter 25

11 Months Later - Foals Are Dying

"Mr. Flannery, this is Dr. Gardot."

"Hello Doc. How'r things going?"

"Interestingly enough, it's not as bad as we'd thought. I mean it's bad, but not as bad as it could be."

"Don't follow ya Doc."

"Not every farm is experiencing this problem. From what we've been able to find out, the stillborns are coming from a very select group of stallions."

"No kidding. Wouldn't have thought that. What about the stallions?"

"That's what we can't figure out. They look fine."

"What can I do?"

"Well, as a matter of fact you can help. Would you mind calling the managers where these stallions are located? I'm sure they'd rather talk to you than me."

"No problem, just tell me when and where."

Gwen assembled her list of stallions before driving out to Fairhaven Farm. Reviewing the list with Tuck, she asked if she could again examine Kissin Kouzins.

"Mr. Flannery, I've never seen anything like this. I mean she's as healthy as any mare I've ever seen."

"Yeah, she'll be ready to breed again in about two weeks."

Healthy mares, on average, produce one foal per year, and are usually bred within 30 to 40 days following delivery.

"Say Doc, would you mind calling me Tuck?"

Gwen stood staring at the mare's hind hoof without replying. Realizing that he might have spoken out of line, Tuck decided to go all the way.

"And do you think you might have dinner with me sometime?"

Not much of a lady's man, he shied a bit after asking her for the date. Not much of a socialite herself, Gwen looked around from the backside of Kissin Kouzins blushing.

"I, ah, well," stumbling for words, and finding herself in an uncomfortable position, she finally managed to blurt, "yeah, I guess so. When did you have in mind?"

"Oh, I don't know. I guess you're pretty busy and all, but how about tomorrow night?"

"Well, okay."

"I'll take you to Merrick Inn. Ever hear of it?"

"Yes I have. That's a pretty nice place. What should I wear?"

"Well, it's according to whether you want to dress up, or just go casual?"

Gwen couldn't believe she was hearing this right. Not being a church goer, she hadn't dressed up since her graduation.

"What do you suggest?" she asked, squinting into the sun, her short blond hair blowing in the breeze above her pretty, freckled face.

"Let's just go casual. I don't like to wear a tie and I don't know where my sport coat is.

It was apparent neither had much of a life outside their individual careers.

Entering the dimly lit bar at Merrick Inn, the following evening, they made their way to one of the round tables along the far wall across from the dark rosewood bar. There was a slight smell of smoke, but not enough to be bothersome. A cheerful, middle-age waitress placed two napkins in front of them before asking for their order.

"I'll have a whiskey sour," said Gwen.

"What do you have on tap?" asked Tuck.

"Bud, Bud Light, Guiness, Sam Adams."

"Guiness," replied Tuck, interrupting her before she could finish naming all the beers.

"Yes sir, and my name is Sherry."

As Tuck's eyes adjusted to the darkness, he noticed the "horse" motif of the famous restaurant, which seemed classier than most of the other local restaurants trying to emulate the Bluegrass and its surroundings.

Merrick Inn was the farm house of the old Merrick Horse Farm, built in the early thirties. In 1961 the farm, located about four miles from downtown Lexington, was sold and developed into an apartment complex, leaving the beautiful farmhouse intact. Each room of the three-story mansion was decorated southern style, as huge candle-lit chandeliers bathed dinner guests in soothing ambience. When the waitress brought their drinks, Tuck raised his glass to Gwen saying, "God bless us everyone."

"You sure are a man of plain words," she joked. "I would have thought you could have come up with one of those Irish toasts like... may you be half an hour in heaven before the devil knows you're dead, or something like that."

"You'd think, but I'm not sure if it's cause I don't remember that well, I drink too much, or I just don't read enough. Probably a little bit of all three. Speaking of words, look at this," said Tuck, pointing to a large picture hanging on the wall next to their table. It was a painting of Secretariat prancing about the paddock prior to running the Belmont in 1973. Triple matted in heather green, deep amber and a very pale yellow, and framed with the picture on the left, there was a poetic calligraphy on the right.

"Man was he some horse?" said Tuck. "Did you see him run any of the Triple Crown races?"

"I saw him run the Derby, but I missed the last two."

"Did you know that when he died his autopsy found that his heart was twice the size of a normal Thoroughbred?"

"I'd never heard that."

"Yeah, he died kind of unexpectedly and I remember how

awful I felt."

I've never seen a painting framed like that. What's the poem say?"

"Hold on, I'll read it to ya."

Tuck moved his chair closer to the painting, squinting his eyes.

"It starts out, Secretariat."

I can still see your colors of checkered blue and white.

Down through my memory's backstretch, on wing's poetic flight.

Your golden hair free flowing, always put the sun to shame.

And every true Kentuckian was branded by your name.

Derby day in Louisville found thirteen horses game.

But with a flash of chestnut lightning, it would never be the same.

They loaded you post number nine - Ron Turcotte high aboard

You broke the gate in dead last place, as the betting gallery roared.

But around the backstretch steady, you unleashed your awesome strength.

Atop the lane, you passed by Sham and won it by two lengths.

What made this feat so special, through the legend and the lore.

You ran each quarter faster than the one you ran before.

The challenge of the Preakness, produced another win.

As you came from last to take the lead from Sham but once again.

And then it was the Belmont, third gem within the crown.

Where hearts are broken, dreams are crushed and has-beens abound.

But this is where you captured fame to set your spirit free.

The sweetness laden Triple Crown and immortality.

You set the pace to hold a place where gods and eagles soar.

To win by lengths of thirty-one; your time, two twenty-four.

The day your huge heart ceased to beat and slipped its earthly place.

I dreamt you pranced across the bar with heaven's holy grace.

To harness for eternity, both you and Man-O-War.

To guide His silver chariot, along His golden shore.

"Beautiful," murmured Gwen, touched by the nostalgia of the great horse. "I like the way the poet attributes Secretariat's beauty to a heavenly place."

"Yeah, I do too. If people only knew just how beautiful these animals truly are, ya know?"

"Yeah, that's why we've gotta cure this thing and quick. Makes me feel guilty that I'm here and not at the lab."

"Hey, everybody needs a break now and then."

"So, have you called anyone?"

"Sure have, let's see, Collis McCovey from Stallion Manor, Hail My Chief is over there. You know, we had Heart Lancer over there last year for a few months. Then we brought him back to Fairhaven."

They talked about the farm managers Tuck had called until he asked, "How about another round, you ready?"

"I'm good for now," said Gwen with a studious look on her face.

"So tell me, why isn't every farm experiencing this problem?"

"I wish I knew," she said, looking around to see if anyone could hear. "That's the million dollar question."

Discussing the need for a meeting of farm managers to be held as soon as possible, Gwen, feeling at ease for the first time in weeks, motioned to the waitress saying...

"You ready? This one's on me."

Feeling better about her life, at least for the moment, she sipped her cocktail, glancing at Tuck out of the corner of her eye thinking how surprised she was that she was enjoying herself so much.

Chapter 26

"You mean to tell me you're not sure? We can't afford to leave that little stone unturned. You have to go back! We can't take the chance," said Jules, following Rajad's disclaimer that he wasn't sure if anyone, outside Karoumi, knew about the nose spray.

"He won't talk. Why would he?" Rajad was trying to justify allowing Jefferson Fairchild, whom he'd never met, to remain alive.

"Why didn't the stupid son of a bitch kill him?"

"He just couldn't do it. You must understand him. He is not like that. He would kill anyone who would hurt me or even you, but he is not a murderer."

"Are you willing to risk everything? Everything over this stupid mistake?"

"It cannot be linked to us. Even if he did talk, he does not know our names."

"All he has to know is that the nose spray is from the Middle East. Everyone would be suspect. Especially you since the research center is here, and so new."

They argued until Rajad was convinced Jules was right, and that Darkside would have to return to Kentucky. No one with knowledge about the nose spray and the infection of the horses could remain alive. Jules, however, was beginning to see the end of her involvement with Rajad. She didn't like the way he'd been treating her, placing her beneath him, as was his custom. He was changing, becoming more argumentative and dominant, and she was nobody's servant.

Darkside didn't much like returning to Kentucky, but he did what was asked of him. He was amazed at the vast connections Rajad had and how easily lives could be bought and sold. It was a windy, rainy day, as he sat flipping through a handful of bills at a table near the back of a truck stop just off

Interstate 75.

"$1,000.00 dollars in tens and twenties. As you wished," said Darkside to the husky red-haired stranger with the Red Man hat, denim jacket and black cowboy boots.

"Why you want him hit, anyhow? I mean, just to satisfy my own curiosity."

"Let us just say that it is due to some unfinished business."

"Don't matter to me no way. Usually don't deal with folks from Iran is all."

"I am not from Iran, but that is not important. You will find that he wears a diamond ring on his left hand, in the shape of a horse's shoe. Bring it to me and you will get the remainder of your money. That is the way I will know that you have been successful."

"I'm always successful. You don't have to worry about that. I'll get the ring. Meet you back here say, day after tomorrow. Say three o'clock. Not many folks here then."

"I will be here."

The gentle breeze wafted through the run-down barn on the edge of the small farm, as Jeff parked his truck under the lean-to attached to the white clapboard house. Cutting the engine, he took a long pull on the Ancient Age bourbon bottle he kept under the seat. Entering the house, he sensed something was out of place, causing the hair on his neck to stand up.

"Who are you?"

The sentence hung in midair, as Jeff stared, wide-eyed at a German Lugar pistol. He didn't hear the second, third, fourth or fifth shots fired into his chest. Falling to the floor, his eyes remained open in a horrified stare, as his lungs froze, uncontrollably holding on to his last breath. As dust curled behind the gray Ford rental car rolling out from behind the barn onto the small two lane road from which it came, Jefferson Fairchild exhaled for the last time.

It was two days before Franke Wilson found the body and called the local police. Shaken and stuttering miserably, it was several minutes before the 911 dispatcher could understand that a murder had taken place.

The story of Jeff's death was hardly a concern to anyone in the Central Kentucky area, but it did pique the curiosity of Johnny Stone.

What could Jefferson Fairchild have done to cause anyone to murder him like that, he thought. For a moment he considered a mob hit, or possibly a jilted lover, but didn't accept either as a reasonable explanation. *But five bullets, all in the heart?*

Chapter 27

Tucker Allen Flannery was born April 17, 1952, just days before Calumet Farm's Hill Gail won the 78th running of the Kentucky Derby. He was the youngest of Hank and Ethel's two children and would have remained that way if not for the auto accident that claimed the life of his older brother, Peter, following his high school senior prom. Two couples, including Peter and his sweetheart Susan, piled into Collin Napier's daddy's Cadillac convertible, along with several pints of peach brandy, and headed out Old Frankfort Pike to one of the several post prom parties. They never made it. After cresting a roller coaster hill at better than eighty miles per hour, Collin lost control, flipping the car several times, killing everyone inside. Young Peter was thrown head first into a large oak tree, requiring his casket to remain closed. Tuck, only 13 then, never saw his brother after that morning's breakfast when he teased him about how funny he was going to look in his tux.

"Hey squirt, you keep that up and you'll never live to wear one. See ya," said Peter, running off to pick up his corsage. Those were the last words Tuck would ever hear him say.

Following Peter's funeral, Tuck became his mother's sole salvation. Ethel doted on him, pouring her love over him as milk over a bowl of cereal. But so often it seems, life, in it's own wicked way, allows tragedy to follow tragedy in a heartless, vicious cycle. It wasn't long after Peter's death that Ethel found herself embroiled in a bitter battle with lung cancer. She and Hank kept it from Tuck as long as they could, but were forced to tell him when she entered St. Joseph's hospital for a radical mastectomy.

That year was particularly tough on Tuck, watching his mother literally die in front of him. Thoughts of her tethered to an oxygen bottle, coughing up phlegm and blood while trying to smoke a cigarette, caused him many sleepless nights.

Although Ethel was a fairly tough person, having enlisted in the Women's Air Corps during WWII where she'd spent fifteen months in the South Pacific identifying enemy planes, she was no match for the ravenous disease that wracked her frail and helpless body. A body that was once strong and full of life.

Ethel was enrolled in the five gait show horse competition at the Kentucky State Fair the summer of 1946, when she and Hank met, and was considered by many in the competition to be the woman to beat. Hank first noticed Ethel dressed in her show jodhpurs, with her long red hair pulled back in a bun under her black derby hat, and was smitten by her handsome features and energetic mannerisms. She was all business when she rode and, to Hank, she was simply poetry in motion.

He was searching his soul for just the right words to introduce himself when he walked back into the horse stalls looking for her that August afternoon. But what happened next was always subject to debate between the two people fated to become lovers. To hear Hank tell it, he just came upon Ethel whipping this sorry excuse for a man with her riding crop. "Hell, she tore that ol boy's shirt to shreds," he'd say whenever he'd relate the story to a neighbor or friend.

It seems that Ethel had been grooming her mount, Jim Bob, for the show gait event, when this arrogant, slightly drunk aristocrat staggered in with a beautiful gelding throwing the reigns at one of the attendants, and leaving the animal without food or water, as he made his way back to the festivities. Ethel and the attendant serviced the horse, and when Ethel gave the animal a drink of water, the gentle gelding drank not only one bucket full, but two. Ethel would later recall how the horse ate like it hadn't eaten in days and how the animal had shown signs of physical abuse. That was all it took to get Ethel's dander up, and when the man came back the next afternoon, she was waiting for him.

"Did you know your horse hadn't had food or water when you just walked out and left him unattended?" she demanded.

"What the hell business is it of yours?" asked the man, in a cold, condescending manner.

To his misfortune, he had said the wrong thing to the wrong person at precisely the wrong time, and Ethel, forgetting her dignity, chased him with her riding crop switching the man completely out of the barn. That's the kind of horse woman Ethel was and she was proud of it.

But those loving memories would be all that Tuck would have of her after she'd lost her battle with cancer toward the end of that year. She struggled through four months of agonizing torture before the angel of mercy came for her one night while Tuck and Hank held vigil by her bed.

She'd been moved from the intensive care unit to a private room where the two of them, along with the night duty nurse, tearfully held hands, as the priest from St. Paul's Catholic Church led them in final prayer. As Ethel Flannery's spirit prepared to leave her devastated body, the blip on the heart monitor machine slowly flat-lined with the pumping noise of the respirator fading softly into the background. Hank gently cradled the love of his life in his arms, whispering tenderly in her ear...

"I will love you forever, Ethie. I will love you forever."

With tears rolling down his ashen cheeks, Hank faced the nurse and said softly...

"I'd like to thank you for everything you did. I wonder if I might see her with all these tubes and hoses removed. I'd like to spend a little time with her before you take her. If that's okay?"

The nurse, in tears herself, said, "Sure. I'll just be a minute. The doctor has to examine her first, but I'll come for you when she's ready. Take all the time you need."

Chapter 28

Not many men can be both mom and dad to a broken hearted young adolescent, but Hank did about as good a job as could be expected. He was a sweet natured man who always had a smile on his face and a kind word, which yielded him a wide range of friends and an honorable reputation. Hank may not have been wealthy, but he paid his debts on time and always had an extra dollar for someone less fortunate than himself. With his many trips to the various tracks around the country, he'd become well known in the horse business, and was very well liked.

Completely devoted to his role of father, he'd spend hour after hour teaching Tuck the specifics of horse training. It was largely due to Hank's patronage and reputation that Tuck was hired by Fairhaven Farm to exercise and walk horses the summer following his sophomore high school year. Tuck worked for Josh Whitely, farm manager at that time, patterning his character after his dad, remaining as cheerful and smiling and easy to be with as possible. As he grew in experience Hank wanted him to branch out and try other jobs, especially after his senior year, but Tuck was treated well at Fairhaven and felt an obligation to stay.

When he was 18, Tuck enrolled at the University of Kentucky where, following two semesters, he'd amassed a 1.8 grade point average, rendering him ineligible to continue until he sat out a semester. It was during this probationary period that he grew the final inch and a half to become an exceptionally strong young man, 6' 1" weighing around 190 pounds. He'd let his sandy hair grow longer than his dad had liked, allowing it to drape over his ears and hang slightly over his left eye. But he kept himself very clean and dressed in clothes that did not distinguish him from most of the farm hands in the county.

"Tuck, you getting yourself ready for school next fall?" asked Hank one evening, as Tuck came through the door for supper.

"I guess so."

"You guess so?"

"I don't know, Dad. Come on, you never went to college."

"Now look, I don't want to hear that again. Your mother and I always," Hank stopped short. He didn't want to put the boy on a guilt trip.

"I know, Mom wanted me to go. But I'm just not ready yet. I can't go to classes when my mind isn't in it. Besides, I want to be a horseman."

"And horsemen don't need an education?"

"I'm just not ready yet, Dad. Maybe in a year or two, huh?"

Hank looked at Tuck with affection and disappointment, as he mashed the hot steaming potatoes. He'd promised Ethel he would see to it that the boy earned his degree, but he just didn't know how to make it happen. He had to find a way, but for now, it was supper time.

"Wash up son, let's eat."

Tuck never did go back to college, although he'd thought about it from time to time. His interest in farm management grew with every bale of straw he'd pitch and every stall he'd muck out. He worked hard for Fairhaven Farm and when Josh Whitely retired, Mrs. Blevins sent for him.

"How do Mrs. Blevins," he said, walking through the tall mahogany doors into her office.

"Come in Tucker, and sit down for a moment. May I offer you a cup of tea? I've had it simmering for quite some time now and it's good," said Audra Blevins, a tall, slender, stoic lady with impeccable snow white hair.

No matter when Audra Blevins was seen in public, she was always dressed in a tailor made colorful suit. Today she'd selected lavender with a creme colored blouse tied with a large bow just under her chin. She was an exceptionally intelligent woman, having earned a bachelor of arts degree in history from Center College in Danville, Kentucky. Her steel gray eyes had a wondrous magnetism which could captivate the devil himself. A Rothchild by birth, she'd married beneath herself, according to blue chip standards, when Charles Wilcock Blevins, a coal operating millionaire, asked for her hand in 1947. With his work ethic and her intellectual influence, the two young equine enthusiasts bought a tract of land 14 miles from Lexington, with the intention of building a horse farm. With the help of Carney Puckett and a few select friends, the farm quickly grew into a modern Thoroughbred training and breeding facility.

Charles and Audra Blevins employed the two basic items necessary to develop a successful horse farm: money and luck, with the emphasis on luck. Fairhaven's luck was a mare they'd acquired in a $5,000.00 claiming race named Cat Dancer who suffered from a breathing malady known as Heaves. Carney Puckett knew Cat Dancer was a speed horse from quality bloodlines, but Heaves, when not treated properly, can severely impair a horse's breathing and, in some cases, cause death. Carney tried an old remedy on Cat Dancer when he placed the horse at the end of the barn and ordered her stall to be completely cleaned, aired out, and strewn with wood chips instead of straw. She was given a daily ration of oats and molasses, and her hay was always soaked in warm water. When the huge bay filly would prep for her morning workout, Carney would coat her tongue and nostrils with Vicks Vapo Rub.

Cat Dancer responded perfectly and trained well enough to win over $200,000.00 dollars the following three years. She was eventually bred to Ghostofadream, a local stallion of notable stamina, producing Dreamer's Wraith the summer of 1960. Dreamer's Wraith, although not a big stakes winner himself, had a way of siring sons and daughters who were. One of the stallion's last offspring, prior to his demise, was a colt out of Cimeronne named Heart Lancer.

Heart Lancer was by all means one of the most heralded horses of his day and was undefeated in his two-year-old campaign, even though he'd raced only four times that year. But, as fate would have it, the beautiful chestnut colt fractured his cannon bone training for the 1986 Kentucky Derby. He returned to the track the following year, but was not the same and could not recapture his juvenile form. Though a failure on the field, he was prolific in the breeding shed, with several stakes winners in his progeny, including sons: Royal Lancer, Catomyran, and Heartofthecat. The fantastic stallion's breeding fees increased, monumentally, each year. The farm was on the rise and doing exceptionally well and Audra Blevins had every intention of maintaining her good fortune, as she sipped her tea leveling her eyes at Tuck.

"Tucker, have you thought about your future? I mean five to ten years from now?"

Although not completely prepared for this encounter, Tuck handled himself with reserved maturity.

"Well, I've always wanted to be a horseman, ma'am. I know I should go back to school, but, that's what my dad wants me to do. I know I should go back, but I'm just not ready."

"You know Tucker, your father is one of the finest people I've ever met. And I know you don't want to disappoint him."

"No ma'am, I sure don't. But I want to do what's best for me. I really like what I'm doing here, I mean I love Fairhaven and well..."

"Tucker, I'll be honest with you. I would never go against your father's wishes for you, but I am very impressed with you as an individual and with your performance. As you know, I am in need of a new farm manager and I'd like to know if you would consider the job?"

Tuck couldn't believe what he'd just heard. He'd never thought about managing Fairhaven Farm. At least, not at this point in his life.

"Umm, gee, well. I guess, if you really want me to manage it. I uh..."

"Tell ya what I'm gonna do. You take a couple of days and think about it. Talk to your father. I'm sure he'll give you some good advice. Let's see, today's Tuesday. Why not let me know by Friday. How's that?"

"Well Mrs. Blevins, I don't know what to say. I guess I'm thankful to you for having the confidence in me. And I sure will let you know by Friday, ma'am."

Chapter 29

Tuck and Hank talked about it for two full evenings before Tuck made up his mind. And in his twenty-second year, Tucker Flannery found himself managing a small but very prestigious horse farm in the heart of Thoroughbred country. Hank was very proud.

But tragedy and the fates were not about to abandon him so quickly. On the Fourth of July weekend of that year, Tuck received a call that, once again, brought him to the brink of despair. He'd been out all day with his friend and fellow horseman Kyle Cooney, when they'd stopped at the Jot-Em-Down store for a sandwich. Tuck always kept the Jot-Em-Down phone number, as well as the number of Fairhaven with his answering service so he could be reached in case of an emergency. Nelson Frisch, owner of the store, caught Tuck's eye, as he and Kyle walked through the old screen door of the small country delicatessen, about six miles north of Lexington.

"Tuck, got a phone call for you about 40 minutes ago from the state boys. Sounded real important. They left me the number here. Why-ontcha use that phone behind the counter."

"Yer kidding me!" said Tuck, reaching for a cold Coke inside the ancient refrigerator.

"No, no joke, I wouldn't kid about a thing like that."

Tuck could see the seriousness in Nelson's face, as he reached behind the counter for the phone.

"Yeah, this is Tucker Flannery, y'all trying to get hold of me?"

"Yes sir, I have a number for you to call in Somerset."

"What happened?" asked Tuck with a strange tone in his voice, causing Nelson and Kyle to look up.

"Sir, you'll have to call this number. I don't have that

information. If you've got a pen, it's,"

"No wait a minute, hold on. Nelson, you got a pen?"

"Right here," handing Tuck the pencil behind his ear.

Tuck looked puzzled, writing the number down on one of the counter napkins. His heart pounded, as he dialed the long distance area code.

"Pulaski County Police Station, can I help you?"

"My name is Tucker Flannery, and I understand you folks have been trying to reach me?"

"Hold please."

After what seemed like an eternity, a soft, quiet masculine voice came on the line, "Mr. Flannery?"

"Yessir."

"Mr. Flannery, this is Sergeant Meadows of the Pulaski County Police, are you Mr. Tucker Allen Flannery?"

"Yessir."

"Is Mr. Henry Allen Flannery your next of kin, sir?"

"He's my daddy."

"Mr. Flannery, I have some unfortunate news for you. Henry Allen Flannery was involved in a boating accident on Cumberland Lake early this morning."

Tuck's blood ran cold, as he asked, "Is he, alright?"

"I regret to inform you sir, that Henry Allen Flannery drowned at approximately 9:45 this morning. His body has been taken to the Pulaski County Morgue."

Tuck dropped the bottle of Coke, trying to keep the phone from crashing to the floor.

"What's up?" asked Nelson, seeing Tuck was in dire straights.

Tuck's face was.

"Sir, will you be able to come to the Pulaski County Morgue and identify the body?"

"I, I, a, I guess so."

"Mr. Flannery, I am truly sorry for your loss, sir."

Tuck turned to Kyle and said, "I gotta go down to Pulaski County. Gotta go get my daddy. He's dead. He's dead, man."

"Come on big guy," said Kyle, placing his arm around Tuck's shoulder, "I'll drive ya."

The floorboards creaked in the front room of the old funeral home, creating a ghostly, uneasy feeling, as visitors and friends walked gingerly about while a symphony of floral fragrance played softly in the background, filling nostrils and tantalizing teary eyes. Tuck stood staring at the shining gray metal casket, while his mind drifted to better days when he would help his dad work their small farm on the southern edge of Bourbon County. Closing his eyes, he could see the early morning fog lying like a white blanket across the lush fields as his dad tendered a young colt into an old iron starting gate he'd kept along side the shelter the two of them had built. Hank was good with horses - he had a gentle, sweet touch. The most impressive thing about Hank was the softness of his voice.

Doc Baich walked up to Tuck and reminded him of how much Hank had meant to him and all the horse owners in the county.

"If I hadn't seen ol' Hank for twenty years, and he called me on the phone, I'd recognize him right off. Shoot, he could sweet talk your mamma outa her church money if he'd a mind to, and you know your mamma. Ain't nobody could talk her outa anything, 'cept yer daddy. I remember when you and he would go to the horse sales at Keeneland all the time. I hope you never forget those times, Tuck. He was one heck of a fine man."

Tuck thought about those times they'd gone to the horse sales and just sat listening to the bark of the auctioneer. How they'd dress up in coats and ties and rub shoulders with the wealth of the nations out behind the show arena where the buyers gathered to view the animals on which they'd bid. Those were the best of times. When the world was full of magic and the simple beauty of his father's guiding light reflecting on and around the majesty of yearling Thoroughbreds. It was his dad who fostered in him the love he'd developed for the Bluegrass and the knowledge that gold could be found in the late summer sky, as the setting sun silhouetted the horses in the surrounding pastures.

He felt that the best years of his life were behind him now, encapsulated in these tender memories, realizing how much his dad meant to him and how much he was going to miss him.

The heavy emptiness was leaden in his stomach, as he prepared to bury the last remaining member of his family. Nothing he'd experienced whether it be love or indifference, hatred or forgiveness, compassion or guilt, compared to the silent roar of loneliness echoing through the hollow confines of his soul.

Warm salty tears flowed down the sides of his grief-stricken face, as he found a seat in the funeral parlor away from the crowd that had gathered around the casket. Pulling several tissues from the box on the table, he dabbed his eyes, looking at the picture of his dad on a small funeral card he held in his hand. On the flip side was a poem the funeral company had suggested be placed on the card.

Father

The pages of my heart you turn
And in so doing, still I yearn
For days when I was sitting on your knee.

And when in memory I allow
To stroll back through what's over now;
Yesteryear so joyful and so free.

I wander sweetly home again
To play the image and pretend;
Your gentle wisdom lights my fostered mind

And yet I only wish I could,
Recapture there, my childhood;
To place my hand in yours just one more time.

Chapter 30

The early October dawn crept through the open windows of the sovereign palace, as Sheik Ahmed lay in his bed sweating and gasping for air. He'd been experiencing shortness of breath and discomfort in his back and arms for several days, but this morning's pain was different. Attempting to stand and calling for assistance, he fell to his knees as his personal attendant rushed to his side. The palace doctor, upon examining the sheikh, ordered him transported to the newly built, yet still unnamed hospital complex, under a cloak of secrecy.

"No one is to know that I am here," breathed the sheikh, as emergency technicians worked over him. Within minutes, they had him hooked to a battery of state-of-the-art monitoring devices. Dr. Kelley Fields, recruited by Efram to head the cardiovascular unit, arrived just as the sheikh's vital signs were being reported. Studying the data for several moments, Dr. Fields approached the sheikh's bed.

"You must not allow my visit to be of common knowledge. I want no one to know that I have been here."

"Your Highness, I will order my staff to remain quiet about your hospitalization. Now, about your health. Your blood pressure is extremely high. How long has it been since you've had a physical?"

"I do not remember. I usually remain in exceptionally good health."

"Have you had any pain or discomfort recently? Difficulty breathing, that sort of thing?"

"Some, but is that not normal for a man of my years?"

"Sir, we must run some additional tests. You may have sustained a mild heart attack."

"I will remain here until midnight only. Then I must go back to the palace. I cannot allow my people to think their leader is unwell."

Dr. Fields looked the sheikh in the eye and said in a very stern voice. "I'm ordering a complete physical for you. Would you rather your people not have their leader at all?"

"Is it that bad, Doctor?"

"It could be. This is nothing to take lightly. I hate to tell you this and especially in this manner, but this is how people die."

Dr. Fields had spent the majority of his professional life dealing with high-powered individuals from all walks of life who, upon being told of their mortality, simply ignored his warnings. He knew he'd have to impress upon the sheikh that if he didn't follow orders, he was gambling with his life.

The sheikh remained in the hospital for two days, at which time a complete physical was performed. Dr. Fields asked Efram to stop by his office, following his nightly visit.

"Your father must have a bypass operation. He has four blocked vessels. I believe we could perform the operation here, but my recommendation is that he go to Mass. General in Boston."

"Is it really that bad?" asked Efram in a meek voice.

"Yes, it's that bad. I can call and make the arrangements. Mass. General is one of the best, he'll be in good hands there."

"Alright Doctor. I will talk to my father and prepare him for the trip. He will not like it, but he will listen to me. How much time do we have?"

"I would proceed as though there were no tomorrow. He's in pretty bad shape. I know he wants to return to the palace, but I really don't want him released."

"I know, but, under the circumstances, he will want to go home before he must leave his country."

"Only if you make sure he rests. I don't want him going back to work, or doing anything strenuous."

"I will do whatever I must. And thank you Doctor. Karoumi is truly blessed by your presence."

Chapter 31

The golden moon lit the evening sky, reflecting beautifully over the serene waters of the Persian Gulf, as Meredith sat by the waterfall lagoon at Solomon's Grill, awaiting Bill's arrival.

Her voice, on the phone, seemed impatient when she'd asked him to meet her at his earliest convenience. He hurried through the remainder of his daily routine before dashing off to the restaurant where she'd said she'd be. Approaching her table, he could hear the cascading water and could see that she was already on her second martini.

"So what's this hot news you wanted to tell me?" he asked innocently. Not waiting for her answer, he teased, "I know it couldn't be gossip, cause you never participate in that indoor sport, so it must be something technical."

Waving at the waitress, he signaled her to replenish Meredith's drink and to bring him the same. Meredith, looking all too serious, frowned as she began.

"Bill, I caught Jules and the prince together in the lab."

"And?"

"I don't know what I must have been thinking, I was just working late the other night and went down to check on her, that's all. But as I got close, you know, near the outer doors, I could hear them. Making love. I know better than to have eavesdropped, but, I just couldn't pull away. They were so loud."

What Bill didn't know was that Meredith couldn't stop thinking about the carnal encounter and the sensual imagery it portrayed. Her own lovemaking had stopped years before when her husband, having sustained a stroke at the untimely age of 45, could not make love to her the remaining years of their marriage. A woman who didn't believe in extramarital affairs she had not allowed herself the benefits of sexual pleasure, yet didn't realize how much she'd missed it over the last several years. Not only was she captivated by her unplanned discovery, but the protective denial with which she'd surrounded her own emotions was unveiling itself with stark realism.

"Did you say anything to them?"

"No, I just stood there listening. But, that's not the worst of it."

Bill's curiosity was increasing by the second.

"I went down there again last night. I know I shouldn't have, but I thought if I could just talk to her, I could."

"What, what? You could what?"

Looking around to ensure that no one was listening her voice changed to a whisper, "I don't know, but I heard her yelling at the prince. She was yelling something like, "Why didn't you have him killed." I can't be sure, but I think they're involved in something sinister."

"Have him killed? You mean murder? Or were they talking about a snake or something?"

"No, she said something about, "When he had the chance." And the prince said that he couldn't do it. The prince said that he, I mean this other guy, should have killed someone, but that he just couldn't do it."

"Did you get any names?"

"Not really, but I had my heart in my throat during most of their conversation. Jules mentioned some kind of spray and how it could be traced to the Gulf because of the research center."

"Traced to the Gulf. What do you suppose that meant?"

"I have no idea, but they did say that the other man would have to go back and finish the job. Jules said that no one with knowledge of the spray or the infection of horses could remain alive."

"That's pretty serious. What'd the prince say?"

"He seemed like he agreed. I mean he didn't argue with

her after that."

Bill stared at the floor for several moments before speaking.

"Do you have any idea when they'll be back? I mean, we need to find out more about this."

"No, I don't and I'm not sure I want to go back. Bill, I don't want to get further involved."

"We have to, Mere. Is there any place we can hide down there and wait for them?"

"God, Bill, what if we got caught? I mean what do you think they'd do to us?"

"Well, we could pretend we're doing the same thing they are. I mean think about it. You and I need someplace to go to be alone. It's the perfect excuse."

Meredith remained quiet, as the waiter brought the drinks Bill had ordered.

"Here's to us, Mere. Damn if you haven't opened a can of worms here."

"Yeah, I know."

"Whaddya say we eat while we talk this through. I'll tell you one thing. I'm beginning to feel young again. I knew you could do it. But I didn't think it would involve murder."

"Hell, Bill. I don't think I have an appetite after this."

Chapter 32

Against doctor's orders and the advice of his eldest son, the sheikh went into his office the morning after his release, only to confirm that his youngest son had been continuing to mismanage his budget. Not wanting to trouble his father, Efram tried to intercede at a meeting with Rajad called by the sheikh. The brothers had been arguing for several minutes outside the royal office when the sheikh, overhearing them, opened his door pleading...

"Please my sons, let us not have this incessant bickering."

"Father, he is allowed so much more money for his hospitals and schools and I am given a pittance of what he receives," yelled Rajad.

"Do you really believe your horses and your equine facility are of the same value as our schools and hospital? If I have led you to believe that my son, I have done you a grave disservice."

The sheikh knew Rajad had labored hard to develop his dream, but thought he was now acting selfishly. Efram, on the other hand, had neither political desires nor selfish goals. And, even though both Efram and the sheikh wanted Rajad to be successful, their priorities remained with the success of the people. Efram, trying to lighten the moment and avoid any further argument said, "Perhaps next year, when the budget is recalculated, we could,"

"To hell with your budget! That is all I ever hear," screamed Rajad feeling that Efram was patronizing him, upstaging him in front of their father.

"Enough!" cried the sheikh. "What must I do to stop this arguing? You must understand, Rajad, that we do not have unlimited funds for you to build everything you want. You must rethink your needs and remain within your budget. These rules do not only apply to you. They apply to us all."

"All except Efram."

"Rajad, my brother, a year will pass quickly. Maybe we can work together and complete your dream."

Of all the things Efram could have said at that precise moment, he picked the one that sent Rajad into a fury. Although Rajad hated his brother, he'd never before disclosed his feelings to the sheikh. Until now.

"You and I will do nothing together, you pilfering bastard." The words were out of his mouth before he realized what he'd said. And to whom.

"Rajad, you will not say that about your brother!" ordered the sheikh.

Realizing he'd gone too far, Rajad stood glaring at Efram without speaking.

"Do you hear me? I demand you answer me!"

The sheikh, with face reddening, and blood pressure rising was, for the first time in front of his sons, about to lose his temper.

Rajad searched for words to respond, but knew he'd finally reached his limit. He had sinned, and in front of his father. He'd acted despicably and he knew it, but his rage and hatred for Efram was overwhelming.

"Rajad, I," said the sheikh, grabbing his chest while falling to the floor.

"Father!" cried Efram kneeling over him. "Go, get help," he ordered Rajad, but Rajad just stood transfixed.

"Rajad, go get help!" ordered Efram a second time.

For the first time in their lives, they were doing something together, not out of brotherly love, but fatherly love. They managed to get the sheikh to the hospital, but not in time to save his life. It was Dr. Fields who'd supervised the Code Blue, but to no avail. As Efram sat motionless, he heard the dreadful news he'd long anticipated, but could not bear.

"We tried everything but," said Dr. Fields, lowering his

head in sorrow.

"Thank you Doctor. And please thank your staff."

"Is there anything I can do?" asked the doctor.

"You have already done what you can. I must now prepare for his funeral."

The exhausted prince bowed before the doctor, and walked slowly out of the hospital toward his awaiting limousine. He began the sorrowful task of announcing to the world that his father, Sheikh Abu bin Ahmed bin Salemn Al-Farouad, was dead.

Chapter 33

The sheikh's remains were dressed in white Arabian fashion and placed inside the mahogany casket he'd had made to match the one made for his wife. He was laid to rest beside her in the tomb he'd built twenty years earlier. His funeral, attended by royalty from every corner of the Middle East, was one of the largest in modern Arabian history. Efram was crowned Sheikh Abu bin Efram bin Salemn Al-Farouad a few days after the final rituals had been observed.

It was due to his sincere love for his father and his people, that Efram was so warmly welcomed into the Republican Council as monarch and new leader of Karoumi. Nervous, but outwardly confident the first time he addressed the council members, he was determined to persevere even though he was clearly and uncharacteristically somber.

"I would like first of all, on behalf of my brother Rajad and our entire family, to thank everyone for your kindness and your expressions of sorrow and love, in the passing of our father and our leader. I am sure that I speak for everyone when I say that he will remain forever in our hearts. We, as a nation, face a difficult challenge, but with Allah's blessings and our common strengths, we will remain true to our endeavors. As we enter a new year, let us not fail to seek our goals in the spirit set forth by our ancestors. Let us each and every one never fail to remain true unto ourselves."

The unfortunate and untimely death of the sheikh had thrown a pall of sadness over everyone in Karoumi, upsetting most individuals' schedules and routines. All except Bill and Meredith. Two days following the royal funeral, they'd discovered an air shaft vent in a bathroom directly above Jules' lab, which had been left incomplete, due to the delay in finishing the base floor. Meredith knew that Jules usually went to the lab between eight and ten in the evening, at which time she and Bill would wait silently in the second floor bathroom.

It was around nine thirty on the fourth night that they heard Rajad and Jules' violent lovemaking, emitting sounds of primal vigor previously unknown to Bill and Meredith.

"What is that?" whispered Meredith.

"Shhhhh, I want to take some notes. I believe I've been doing it wrong all these years," teased Bill.

"Wonder if they'll talk or just make love?"

After what seemed like an eternity, Jules and Rajad began to converse. Their lovemaking had become void of tenderness lately, and Rajad was beginning to notice a change in the way she looked at him, almost as though she hated him. After climaxing, she didn't want to lie in his arms as she did when they first began their love affair. Now all she wanted to do was jump up and get dressed.

"Why are you in such a hurry?" he asked.

"What difference does it make? I'm satisfied, aren't you?"

"I am always satisfied, but must you be in such a hurry?"

They were interrupted by the sound of Rajad's beeper. Grabbing the laboratory phone, he quickly punched the numbers and, in a stern voice, gave instructions.

"Trans Atlantic! First class! Through Rome? Yes! I must know by tomorrow night! Of course, but I will meet with you then! I do not want to discuss this now! Bring that to me then!"

Jules' mind raced, wondering what was going on with Trans Atlantic.

"Are you going to Rome?"

"It is of no concern of yours."

"Okay, what about what's his name? Have you attended to that yet? Has he been eliminated, or is that no concern of mine as well?"

"I am not prepared to discuss this tonight."

"What the hell does that mean? I'm involved too, you know."

Rajad's infamous temper was about to explode. With a wild-eyed look and contempt in his voice she'd never heard before, he roared. "Did I not tell you I was not going to discuss this?" And without thinking, he slapped her across the face with the back of his hand.

Enraged, she screamed, "Get out of here. Get the hell out of here you son of a bitch."

"No one tells me what to do," he bellowed, hitting her again and knocking her to her knees. "I do what I want, do you understand?"

Picking up a large glass beaker, he threw it against the concrete wall, shattering it all over the floor. Standing over her sneering, he gathered a handful of her hair pulling her head back saying, "You belong to me. You will do as I say! When I say! Is that clear?"

Shoving her back to the floor, he stormed out of the lab.

Bill and Meredith sat motionless, neither of them having drawn a breath for over a minute.

"Damn!" said Bill. "I think Jules has bitten off more than she can chew."

"I've got to do something, Bill. I can't let him get away with that."

"You can't show your hand yet, Mere."

"Well, I can't let him treat her like that."

"Let it ride for a day or two. Maybe he'll cool down and everything will blow over."

"I just think she's in over her head."

"Yeah, but she's not alone. There's lots of women in that situation."

"I know, but she's on my staff." Meredith was extremely disturbed.

"And mine too, Mere. Hell, I brought her here. But she's a pretty savvy girl and if I know her, I wouldn't want to be in his shoes right now."

"What do you mean?"

"Just a feeling. I know one thing. Jules Weherner can take

care of herself. I sure as hell wouldn't want to cross her," said Bill, as though he knew something about Jules that Meredith did not.

The following day, Meredith casually stopped by the library, asking for Jules.

"Oh, Dr. Pehlagrem, she called in sick today."

"Did she say what was wrong?"

"I believe she said she'd been cramping and didn't sleep well last night."

"Thank you, dear. She'll probably feel better tomorrow."

The following day, Meredith again dropped by the library and could see that Jules was favoring a swollen lip.

"Hello Jules, I heard you were out sick yesterday, so I thought about stopping by today to see how you're doing. Everything okay?"

"Oh, fine Doctor. I just had a bad day yesterday, but today everything's much better."

"What happened to your lip?"

"Oh that. Sometimes when my body retains water, my lips swell. Kinda weird, huh?"

"Well, I guess we all have a bit of weird in us. I hope you feel better though."

"Thank you, Doctor. I do."

Within minutes, Meredith was on the phone to Bill telling him that Jules had, indeed, been slapped in the face.

"How bad is it?"

"Well, it was bad enough for her not to come into work yesterday. Her lip is a little swollen, that's all."

"When do you think they'll get together again?"

"My guess is, it'll be a few days. He's got to cool off and her swelling needs to go down. Probably a week."

"Okay, I'll see you later this evening, then. We can plan it from there."

"It will have to be late, I've got a staff meeting at six."

"Okay, eight o'clock. How's that?"

"You got it. See you then."

Chapter 34

Rajad knew that there was no way he could continue as Prince of Karoumi under the leadership and command of his older brother. But he also knew that he could not allow the cowardly deed of killing Efram to include his closest confident. Mostly because he realized that Darkside, unable to eliminate Jeff Fairchild himself, had more of a conscience than he'd expected. No, it was his Turkish acquaintances who were, once again, called upon to administer this task. And it had to be done quickly, before Efram could gain control of his spending.

He knew Efram was planning a trip to the United States in December, and, through his conniving ways and secret associates, he also knew Efram's travels would take him across the Atlantic aboard Flight 718 from New York to Rome, on his return leg. Through his Turkish cohorts he was able to procure the device which would bring an end to his brother's life and a new beginning to his own.

It would cost him two million American dollars to have the package placed aboard the plane, but, in his mind, it was money well spent. He stayed within the confines of his suite of rooms that night, awaiting the report of Flight 718's demise, but when it never came, the sadistic prince thought he'd been double-crossed.

He was consumed with greed, power and confusion, as he paced the floor wondering why they hadn't reported that the plane had gone down. He slowly realized he'd been betrayed and there was nothing he could do about it.

After a refreshing three days in Rome, Efram returned to Karoumi amidst a fanfare of royal welcome. This was the first homecoming in his new role as sheikh, and he wasn't completely sure how to feel about it. He loved his people, but was uncomfortable with all the publicity he was accorded.

Among the many servants and staff greeting him that day was a tall man with a large birthmark on his cheek. Efram knew of Darkside, but also knew of his complete devotion to Rajad, which caused Efram to wonder why the handsome man would be among the official reception corps. Looking into Darkside's eyes, and watching him bow before him did, however, bring an instantaneous feeling of peace to the young sheikh.

These were troubling times in many ways, and Efram knew that his brother hated him. He also felt alone in the world, having lost the only person who could counsel him wisely. Nevertheless he knew he must take command of his country and his world, and could not afford to wallow in self-pity.

Rajad, on the other hand, had to know what happened aboard Flight 718 and why it had not exploded. He called on his only true friend, the only soul he could trust.

"I have a job for you."

"Whatever you desire, my Prince." said Darkside.

"Go to Istanbul. I must know what happened. I will pay you well for this my friend."

"As you wish, Sire. As you wish."

Darkside left late that night aboard a small jet the royal family used for official business. He made contact with Rajad's Turkish underground associates, but was unable to obtain the information Rajad was seeking.

Thinking the bomb a failure, Rajad now felt double-crossed, and he knew he could never fully trust these Arabian terrorists. Not in the business of planting bombs on planes and destroying lives. His world was closing in now that his brother was the head of state, and his lover's avoidance was gnawing at him. He felt trapped by his own despicable actions, and didn't know what to do. He figured his only way out was through Jules. He would have to rekindle their relationship, and seek another way to rid himself of his brother, while maintaining mastery of his world.

He and Jules could start a new year together. That's what

he'd use to relieve his mind of the wrongs done to him. He would wine and dine her and treat her like his queen.

That's it, he thought. *I will propose marriage. I will keep her with me at any cost.*

Chapter 35

Deciding he'd had enough of Karoumi's restaurants for awhile, Bill had invited Meredith to dine with him at his apartment. He'd baked a leg of lamb, made a tossed salad, a fresh fruit salad, and had topped things off with a bottle of fine Merlot. After dinner, the two moved out to the small covered patio overlooking the edge of the municipal park.

"This is pleasant, Bill. Your place is so much nicer than mine."

"Only because I've decorated it. Why don't you decorate yours? I'll help you."

"You're right. I should. It's just that I never seem to find the time or energy. It's just not something I find important enough to make time for. I think we've," she hesitated, a frown overtaking her face.

"What's the matter?" he asked, leaving his chair and placing his arms around her shoulders. "Something's been bothering you all evening. What is it?"

She began to cry. She knew she was falling in love with him, and she felt guilty about it. Yet she knew she couldn't tell him, it would just make matters worse.

Sensing the dam of feelings between them was about to burst, he knew that their time was at hand. He Lifted her tear-streamed face, placing his lips tenderly against hers, kissing her passionately.

"I love you, Mere."

Reaching up and placing her arms around his neck, she said, "Oh Bill, I love you. I love you. I know I shouldn't, but I do. God forgive me, but I love you."

Their friendship was honed from a mutual admiration for each other's character, and they shared an affinity for their chosen field; the love and care of horses. They realized that their time was now, and that it was meant to be.

Their lovemaking that first night was awkward, as both had been without passion for such a long time. But with Bill's lightheartedness, they stumbled through the early moments, lying in each other's arms, kissing and snuggling until the pale dawn blessed them, chasing the shadows of night back into its empty cage.

"What do we do now?" she asked. "I mean, about your marriage?"

"I'm married in name only. We talked about divorce before I decided to come here. We felt that some time away from each other might rekindle our love, but, it's not going to happen, Mere. I'm going to insist on a divorce."

"Are you sure, Bill? Are you really sure that's what you want?"

"I want you Mere. If you'll have me?"

"You know I will, but I don't want to be the cause of your divorce."

"Ha, that's a laugh. We haven't had a marriage in years. I'm not sure we ever did, but I'm not going to say anything against her. I just want out."

"Are you sure, Bill? Really sure?"

"I'm sure, but what about you? I mean are you happy? I mean really happy, like before?"

"Before?"

"When you were married. You know before the accident."

Meredith never talked about the accident, and she was very partial with whom she shared the tragedy. But she remembered when she and Jonas were very happy in the days before the head-on collision that claimed the life of their only child Sarah age 11, and left the man she loved paralyzed from the neck down.

Every day for five years, Meredith, and a private nurse, bathed, clothed and feed Jonas before she would have to go to work. She tried maintaining a positive attitude until the morning Jonas told her that he didn't want to live any longer. He just wanted to go on and leave his body. But the devastation of his despair and the fact that he wanted to leave her behind, pushed her close the edge, wrecking not only her happiness, but nearly destroying her emotionally as well. Although outwardly undetectable, she hadn't been happy in a very long time. Not until recently. Not until Bill.

"I'm happy with you, Bill. And I love you."

"I love you too, Mere."

Chapter 36

Jenny Stromquist was a blond haired, brown eyed 98 pound 26 year old waif in jodhpurs, who could ride the wind if you could put a saddle on it. She was the illegitimate daughter of Sadie Stromquist, a back-alley tramp who would stoop to any level to earn a measly living, just inside the poverty line. As long as Sadie had her fill of life's basic needs, booze and cigarettes, she was content.

Jenny had spent the better part of her childhood passed around to anyone who'd baby-sit her, while her mother earned what little money she could, turning tricks out of some of Louisville's sleazier bars and hotels. To say that Sadie was a hard working single parent, raising a child alone in a harsh world, doing the best she could with what she'd had to work with, would be an abomination. Sadie was a cheap slut. On one occasion, she forced Jenny into the trunk of a car, so she and a local farm worker could have their way in the backseat.

"Jenny, wake up, you gotta git in the trunk."

"Mommy no!" cried the seven year old, as her mother pulled her out of the backseat.

"Now shut up and get in there goddamit so I won't have to slap the tar out a ya."

The scared little girl spent the next half-hour in the dirty, cramped trunk of a 1962 Buick, listening to her mother and a man she hardly knew cavort disgustingly in a vile and lust-filled manner.

Incidents like that plagued Jenny's childhood, causing her to run from her trailer park home and pool hall lifestyle. She found refuge working the barns and fields of Kentucky's Thoroughbred industry when she was just 14 years old. Her first home was a bale of straw in the vacant stall of a nearby horse barn, until she was gradually upgraded to a cot in the corner of the barn office. Her passion, however, was a hand full of mane while perched bareback aboard one of nature's fleetest animals, as she'd often do late at night when no one was around to see her.

By the time she was 18 she was an accomplished rider, afraid of nothing and able to hold her own with any of the men she worked with. Nothing she'd experienced came close to the exhilaration she felt atop a 1,000 pounds of explosive energy, as she exercised the horses early each morning.

The best thing in her life was that happenstance had brought her to Fairhaven Farm at the early age of 15, where she began working for Tucker Flannery. With Tuck's friendship and tenderness and Carney Puckett's tutelage, Jenny maintained a daily workout on the best Thoroughbreds Fairhaven had to offer. From the day she started she'd maintained a crush on Tuck, but he always kept her at bay with his brotherly attitude. He liked Jenny, but not in a romantic way. And Tuck was a gentleman.

"I saw you lookin' at my butt, now come on admit it," said Jenny, as Tuck gave her a leg up one morning.

"Look, you just keep your mind on business or this ol boy'll throw you through next week."

"Hell, you ain't man enough for me no how."

"Maybe not, but this gelding sure is and you better keep yer mind on business. Now let's see if you're man enough to ride him."

"Son, if you can saddle 'em, I can ride 'em and I ain't no man. Or don't that matter to you?"

"Don't you worry about that, you've got enough to worry about right here. Just keep him from running out too fast," said Tuck slapping the rump of Jenny's mount. "Hell, you might even get a ride this meet, if it don't rain hard and the creek don't swell."

It was the fall meet at Keeneland Racetrack in Lexington, where Jenny got her start. Carney placed her on Juliet's Pride, a maiden three-year-old filly, to run in the second claiming race that cold, overcast October afternoon. She managed to bring the young horse from a bad start to finish second in a six furlong race including eight other horses, all ridden by men. From that moment on, her status at Fairhaven changed; she was now a jockey.

Her first two seasons she rode for Fairhaven exclusively, but in her third year, as her popularity increased, she hit the circuit. By the time she was 22 years old, she was one of the mainstream riders, hovering just below the big boys and anxious for a top ride. That ride came in the Cambrian Stakes aboard Junior's Lightning, a dynamite two-year-old colt out of California. Jenny received a call from the horse's owner, C.J. Blackford, shortly after he'd seen her ride at Churchill Downs that summer.

Normally, a horse's trainer, in conjunction with the owner, makes the call as to who will ride the mount, but C.J. Blackford did not consult with anyone when selecting his jockey. He made his fortune the hard way, without help from anyone, and when it came to making decisions, he was a party of one. Calling Jenny from San Francisco, he asked, "How'd ja like to ride for me, kid?"

"Whadda ya got?"

"I've got lightning in a bottle, kid. Think you can ride my colt in the Cambrian? He's ornery as hell, but I believe you might handle 'em."

Jenny couldn't believe her ears. She'd been waiting for her chance at the big money and here it was.

"Yes sir, I can handle him," knowing she'd better sound cocky.

"I'm gonna be in Lexington on the 24th. I'll see you then."

"Yes sir Mr. Blackford, and thank you sir. You won't regret this."

"No problem, kid. Take care."

The Cambrian Stakes a $200,000.00 contest run early in February is considered a reasonable test for young horses beginning their three-year-old campaign. How well a two-year-old Thoroughbred finished the first year of racing usually dictated which direction it would go the following spring. Many horses like Junior's Lightning would be placed in one or more of the Kentucky Derby prep races, based on her or his performance.

Jenny rode Junior's Lightning in the Cambrian finishing third, closing on the favorite at the wire. She knew she could have won the race if she'd not allowed herself to get boxed inside at the head of the lane. With the amount of horse she finished with, she knew the next race would be hers, that is if she was allowed to ride him again.

"Not bad, kid," said C. J., as he approached Jenny just outside the jockey's lounge.

With her mud caked goggles on top of her head and her face stained a dark brown, the waif-like jockey said, "No sir, we could have won, I know it. We got trapped and it just wasn't there, but he ran great, Mr. Blackford. He ran great. You got a good horse there."

"Yeah, I saw him. He's got the stuff alright. Look, kid. I liked the way you sat him today. If he's ready for one of the Derby preps this spring, I'm gonna let you ride him. Think you can do that for me?"

"I'll ride him, Mr. Blackford. I'll ride him. And we're gonna win."

"I like your style kid, I'll be in touch."

Chapter 37

As the season progressed, Junior's Lightning trained for the Gotham Stakes, a mile race run in the middle of March. But, as race day approached, Blackford had second thoughts about Jenny. He pulled her from the mount in favor of a more experienced rider, much to Jenny's chagrin and the disappointment of Johnny Stone and the rest of the racing world.

Johnny thought Jenny had gotten a raw deal and wrote about it in one of his columns, claiming that Jenny was pulled from the mount because she was a woman. He faulted C.J. Blackford and horsemen like him, questioning them how women were to gain the necessary experience to compete with their male counterparts if they were continually denied equal opportunity. After watching Jenny ride, over the past several meets, Johnny felt she'd earned the mount.

Johnny's article did further Jenny's cause though, as she was featured in the April issue of Horse and Track magazine. On an afternoon just days after the monthly periodical hit the news stands, Johnny called Fairhaven Farm looking for information.

"Mr. Flannery, this is Johnny Stone of the Herald Leader, I wonder if I might stop by this afternoon? If you wouldn't mind, I'd like to talk to you."

"Well, I'm always on the run around here, but hell, why not. By the way, I liked what you wrote about Jenny Stromquist. That was a nice article and it sure helped her career."

"Thanks, but you don't have to thank me, I mean that gal should never have been pulled from that mount. That still pisses me off."

"Yeah," said Tuck. "It does me too. Sure, come on over, I'll be here."

As the noon day sun cascaded brightly across the lush fence-lined greenery, Johnny Stone pulled his navy blue Coupe Deville onto the pin oak tree-lined road leading up to the main barn and office of Fairhaven Farm. No matter what the assignment, Johnny knew that nothing compared to a ride out into Lexington's surrounding countryside. A cool breeze wafted through the trees, mussing his hair, as he walked up to the barn. Tuck waved to Johnny, seeing the newsman approaching.

"Hello there Mr. Stone, how are you?"

"Fine sir, fine and howbout yourself?"

"Well, that's debatable, but I guess we're doing alright. And this is Doctor Gardot from the research center."

"How do you do, Doctor?"

Unable to restrain herself, Gwen seized the moment.

"Mr. Stone, I've read some of your 'sponging' articles recently and I must say, you have quite a bit of knowledge about a subject that no one seems to know much about."

"I'm not sure I know what you mean."

"I mean, the horse industry doesn't need so much negative exposure. And 'sponging' is just about the most disgusting thing I've ever heard of."

"Well, I'm sorry you feel that way, and I have to agree with you, but reporting that and things like it is how I earn my living."

Realizing Johnny'd been bushwhacked, Tuck quickly cut in, "Mr. Stone, you wanted to ask me some questions?"

"Well, yeah, I've heard some rumors, you know, and I just thought you might shed a little light on them."

"What kind of rumors?"

"I've just heard there's been a problem with newborns this season."

"What sort of problem, Mr. Stone?" asked Gwen, cagingly.

"Well, foals with birth defects, you know, that kinda stuff."

"Where'd ja hear that?" asked Tuck, after a long moment of silence.

"Just some talk around the track and places, that's all."

"You know printing that stuff about 'sponging' sure didn't do anybody any favors," said Tuck.

"Look, I hate it as much as you do. Do you think I should ignore it? I mean, what if it's true?"

"So, let's see if I understand this," said Tuck. "You want me to tell you about another problem you think we might be having so you can continue writing about it? Is that what you're after?"

Johnny knew the way they were reacting, the rumors were probably true. Either that, or these were two of the most sensitive people he'd ever met. He also wondered why a doctor from the research center would be at Fairhaven Farm. But for the moment he was on a quest for knowledge and didn't want to leave empty handed.

"No, not exactly. Hell I grew up around here. I just want to know what's going on."

Tuck looked at Johnny with an expressionless face for what seemed like an eternity before gazing off saying, "We've got a problem."

"Tucker!" snapped Gwen.

"Look, if I let you in on this, we've gotta have your word that you won't print anything until we give you the go ahead. Is that understood?"

"Guaranteed."

"And I'm sure we can trust you," said Gwen, sarcastically.

"No, I don't work that way. If I give you my word I'll hold a story, I won't release it."

"What about your cohorts? Do they follow the same rules? What if one of them gets hold of it and prints it?" Gwen was growing angry.

"Absolutely not. I don't let anyone else in on my stories until I write them."

Johnny was becoming defensive, but in a cool manner.

"If I operated that way, I wouldn't last very long."

Tuck looked at Gwen and looking down at the ground kicked a stick out of the way.

"Okay, Mr. Stone, I'll level with ya. We're approaching a crisis and we don't have a solution. We've had several stillborns and we simply don't know why."

"And that's exactly why you can't print anything," said Gwen. "Because we really don't know why."

"So, what's being done?"

"That's what we were just discussing."

"You mean you have no idea as to the cause?" Johnny couldn't believe his ears.

Neither Tuck nor Gwen responded. Tuck looked at Gwen who'd placed her hand over her eyes, gazing off into the sun.

"How long has this been going on?"

"Best we can tell, about five weeks or so."

"Is there anything I can do?"

"Just don't print anything," said Gwen. "Or at least until we give you the go ahead. Can we count on that Mr. Stone?"

"Fair enough, but I get the story. Deal?"

"Sure thing," said Tuck, he and Gwen both nodding their heads.

Driving back to his office, Johnny knew he'd have to come up with something to keep Sam off his back. He didn't trust his energetic boss from forcing him to write about the rumors. The sweet smell of spring tugged at his thoughts reminding him that this was the best time to be in the Bluegrass, as flowers bloomed, birds chirped, bees hummed, lovers kissed and horsemen the world over headed for Louisville. It was almost Derby time.

But, babies were dying, and he was very sad.

Chapter 38

The dawning sun reflected perfectly from the grandstand windows, framing the stately twin spires in mirror-like fashion. Johnny parked inside gate four enroute to Churchill Downs' famous Backside, where horses were stabled to run the spring meet and the world renowned 1996 Derby classic. Thoroughbreds were already heading for their morning workout, as stable hands mucked stalls and wrapped forelocks. It was April 27th, and the excitement in the air, just eight days before the race, was electric.

Since 1967, the year Proud Clarion, a 30 to one long-shot, won the Run For The Roses, the same year the Hell's Angels threatened to ride out on the track, and the same year Martin Luther King came to town, stirring enough racial tension to cause a small riot, this time of year never failed to raise Johnny's blood pressure. At 22, he and some college classmates decided to visit downtown Louisville the night before that Derby. They all stayed at Bruce Milner's house for the weekend, all but Johnny, that is. Seeing a short fat cop walking with a tall skinny one, and attempting to show-off in front of his chums, Johnny yelled, "Car 54 where are you?" as they strolled up Fourth Street, one block from the increasingly hostile crowd.

On one side of Market Street, just 60 yards away, stood several hundred of Louisville's African American community. Across the street were several hundred of Louisville's white community, each with different viewpoints regarding racial equality. Occasionally, a bottle or brick was lobbed from one side of the street to the other, while the only element of resistance standing between the two hate-filled masses was a line of nerve-wracked, weapon laden policemen, sporting white helmets and very large black clubs.

No sooner had the words left Johnny's mouth than he was

seized, lifted off the ground and carried to a paddy wagon parked around the corner, his feet dangling all the way.

"Wait, wait, I didn't mean it. What are you doing?"

"Hell boy," said one of the cops, "yer drunk."

"Drunk? I am not drunk."

With that, the cops unexpectedly released their hold on Johnny, causing him to stumble slightly.

"You're drunk son. But, you've got the rest of the night to sober up."

Johnny'd spent the night as a guest of the city of Louisville, although not as welcome as most visitors. He, along with 75 other unfortunate souls, whose only crime was appearing at the wrong place at the wrong time and, in Johnny's case, a lack of knowledge as to when to keep one's mouth shut, spent the night crammed into a tiny, smelly cell. With his buddies' collective money, they managed to pay his fine the following afternoon and hop a bus to the track, just in time for the famous race.

Allowing his mind to roam back to that rain-drenched day 30 years before, memories of an infield awash in naked bodies, beer kegs and mint juleps flooded in, like the infield men's room, ankle deep in urine from a disorderly and overflow crowd. He'd remembered a blonde from D.C. who'd snuggled close to him under a blanket they held over their heads, while catching only a glimpse of the rain soaked, mud splattered field, charging the stretch in the most exciting two minutes in sports. That was his introduction to the Kentucky Derby.

"Hey Johnny," said a writer for a local Louisville newspaper, with whom Johnny had often bantered while covering the races.

"Moj, whadda ya know?"

"Hell, can't say it if I do. How've you been? Haven't seen you in awhile."

"Not too bad, not too bad. So, give me the scoop. Who's looking good out there?"

"Aw, I don't know. I kinda like Unbridled Song. That's

him over there and he's just about to go out. He's the favorite. Who do you like?"

"You know Moj, I never try and pick 'em anymore. Just like to come for the aesthetic value."

"Nope. I ain't buyin' that. No kidding who you got?"

"Like the looks of that Cavonnier. Saw him over at barn twelve. Man he's a big colt."

"Yeah he is. Looks like we're gonna have a good day out here. Have you spent much time at Keeneland?"

"Just about every afternoon. Why do ya think I keep this job?"

"Say, you remember when the Bluegrass ran on Thursday?"

"Yeah, sure wish they hadn't changed it."

"Yeah, me too."

The Bluegrass stakes is a Derby prep race run at Keeneland Racetrack three weeks prior to the Kentucky Derby, on the same weekend as the Arkansas Derby and the Wood Memorial.

"Have you heard any good rumors lately?" asked Johnny.

"No, can't say as I have. How 'bout you?"

"Naaaaa. Nothing I can write about."

"Well, stay well, my friend. See ya Derby day."

Leaving Churchill Downs, Johnny felt empty-handed, as he drove back to Lexington. Although surrounded by the majesty of the Derby, he wouldn't allow his mind to wander far because he was on a mission to find what he'd need to write his latest story. A story about what might cause the sport of kings to produce a plethora of stillborn foals. He wasn't sure of his next move since he hadn't heard from Tucker Flannery or that doctor he'd met at Fairhaven.

He was sitting in his office when Sam Stroub stuck his head in the door.

"So, how's it going?" he asked, sipping a large mug of steaming coffee.

Johnny knew what Sam wanted, but realized he had to

stall him.

"Well, looks like Unbridled Song's gonna be the favorite."

"No, not that, the rumors. You know, the stillborns."

"Aaaa, don't know anything yet. Went to Louisville yesterday but was unsuccessful."

"So, maybe that's a good sign. Did ya get your invitation yet?"

"To what?"

"Callie Collquit's party."

"Ha, don'tcha just wish. Now you talk about rumors. That's where I could pick up a good one. Or start one. Wouldn't you like to be a fly on the wall at that place?"

"Would I. Think you could get us an invitation?"

"Are you crazy? I'd bet Bill Clinton couldn't even get in there. Though he'd fit right in."

"If rumors is what you want, then that's the place to go. Too bad you can't finagle a ticket," said Sam half kidding and half serious. "Well anyway, keep me posted."

Chapter 39

The Kentucky Derby is not so much a horse race, although considered the most exciting two minutes in sports, as it is a festival of events covering three weeks of activity. Included in the festivities is one of the world's largest pyro-technical displays, Thunder over Louisville, a hot-air balloon race, a steamboat race, and the $500,000.00 Oaks Stakes race for three-year-old fillies run the day before the Derby. But the real claim to fame is what's known as Millionaire's Row, where the world's hottest actors, country music stars, sports figures, dignitaries, politicians, oil barrens, soothsayers and Indian chiefs attend the famed Derby eve parties.

If some of the Derby eve parties are considered a walk on the wild side, Callie Collquit's party is downright debauchery. Rumor has it that Callie will go to any length or depth to fulfill the most raunchy request and in her own words, "My party usually separates the men from the boys, the girls from the toys and the devil from the deep blue sea."

Always dressed for the occasion, with flowing red hair and the tops of her voluptuous breasts exposed, Callie remains the center of attention as the evening unfolds. A former employee of the infamous Pauline's, a house of ill repute in the western part of the state, she learned how to provide the utmost in worldly pleasure while remaining on the right side of the law. A fabulous hostess, she greets every attendee personally, and hands each one a small leather bag containing a package of glow-in-the-dark condoms, a large marijuana joint dipped in opium, and a small vial of pure, uncut cocaine.

If you are one of Callie's special friends, she might even give you a key you can use to gain entrance to the lower extremities of her 28 room mansion, where a live band of hand-picked musicians can be found playing blindfolded in a huge room lit only by black lights and candles. In front of the band, on a beautiful Persian carpet lie several large water filled mattresses upon which a sea of naked, writhing, oil sprayed bodies immerse themselves in erotic pleasure. Upon each wall a soundless pornographic movie displays slow motion scenes of every sexual act known to man. With Callie's instructions, the band plays slow rhythmic pelvis pumping music, heavily laden with garish saxophones and pagan-like drums.

It doesn't matter your particular sexual preference, anything and everything can be found within the walls of Callie's place. And by the time the grandfather clock in her huge living room strikes twelve, it's safe to say that everyone is having a damn good time.

The only problem folks have following Callie's party is how to get sufficient rest before driving to Louisville in time for the Kentucky Derby. However, Callie sees to it that each leather bag also includes a little black capsule, which guarantees one will remain alert for the entire Derby experience. Coming down from one of Callie's parties is a week long affair, but oh, what a memory.

Chapter 40

The smell of fresh horse manure can overtake one's nostrils with surprising speed, symphonizing into pastoral ambiance more quickly than its arrival, reminding its benefactor of yesteryear and the glorious scent of days gone by. Churchill Downs' famous Backside had once again captured Johnny's attention, as the crowd of more than 135,000 converged on the racetrack. Johnny stood like a kid in a candy store, listening to the interviews given by the nervous, tight-jawed trainers, watching over their charges like mother hens.

Walking from one barn to the next, he grew more nervous and excited with every story he heard. He knew it would take about 20 minutes to walk to the press area near the clubhouse turn, where he'd watched the last several Derbies, but he could not bring himself to leave the horses. The sight of a young, bold three-year-old colt, the sunlight dancing off his gleaming, sweating coat, was breathtaking.

As the afternoon passed, trainers, grooms, and walkers gathered the necessary saddles, blankets and miscellaneous equine regalia and began walking the horses the quarter mile to the paddock where awaited 19 of the world's most successful jockeys to ride the 122nd Run For The Roses. Johnny trailed just behind Bob Baffert and Cavonnier before leaving the group, making his way to the press area.

"Hey Johnny," said a Herald Leader photographer, "where ya been?"

"Backside. Just love it over there. You heading to the track?" Photographers usually move down near the clubhouse turn just before the race.

"Yeah, gotta go. Who ya pickin'?"

"Cavonnier. But don't quote me. By the way, has ABC cut in yet?"

"They're just about to switch over. Gotta go."

It took the better part of an hour for the horses to be saddled and prepped before the paddock manager ordered, "riders up."

Johnny peered through his binoculars, as the horses made their way from the paddock out through the tunnel, filing down past the University of Louisville Marching Band, as the first sounds of Steven Foster's My Old Kentucky Home could be heard. No matter how many times he'd heard the song, the haunting sounds of "The sun shines bright on my old Kentucky home," always brought a tear to his eye and a catch in his throat.

"Unbridled Song is the favorite at 7 to 2 and here we go, they're at the post," said Al Michaels, the ABC announcer, as the last of the field of 19 Thoroughbreds was loaded into the starting gate.

"And they're off..."

Grindstone

From my home in Overbrook, the farm where I was born
To Churchill Downs May 96, as bugler blew his horn.
I was bred from legacy - Unbridled as my sire.
Wayne Lukas honed my every move and molded me with fire.

I left the post from gate fifteen - Jerry Bailey on my back
And gained the clubhouse turn so far behind the favored pack.
Stalking leaders skillfully, we down the backstretch flew.
Our colors blazing gallantly, green and white and blue.

With Cavonnier in second place and Prince Of Thieves to show,
We stormed the outside avenue and won it by a nose.
My heartbeat robbing thunder and my muscles raging free,
Had captured Heaven's trophy and immortality.

My gleaming coat shone brightly as we gained the winner's deck.
Bluegrass pride rained down on me, while roses draped my neck.
Kentucky will remember me and hold me in her grace,
As I will live forever having won her noble race.

Driving East on I-64 toward Lexington to write the story of Grindstone's Derby victory and all that went with it, Johnny couldn't concentrate as thoughts of bloodlines and stillborns plagued him. When he hadn't heard from Dr. Gardot by Wednesday, he decided to call, but hearing only her phone message, he left one of his own.

"Dr. Gardot, this is Johnny Stone. I've got a problem here. I haven't heard from you and I'm having a difficult time keeping the powers that be off my back. My boss says we've gotta run the story. I really need to talk to you."

Gwen dialed Tuck's number knowing full well she was no closer to an answer than when she'd started. Life hadn't prepared her for this. Even though she was an intellectual, she was no prophet. As the call went through, a warm, familiar voice responded. "Hello, this is Tuck."

"Tuck, Mr. Stone says he's gonna print the story."

"He can't do that, he gave his word."

"He called today to say his boss was after him to run it. Something tells me he won't print the whole thing, but I really don't know what to expect."

"Guess we'll just have to brace for the worse. I mean what else can we do? Gotten any further on your research?"

Tuck hadn't been pushing Gwen because he knew she'd tell him if and when she knew something. But he also was somewhat disappointed that, with all the technology and money spent on horses, the research center was no closer to an answer.

"We've been able to rule a few things out, but no... no definitive answer as yet."

"Well, maybe you should call him back and talk with him. Just tell him the truth."

"Whose side are you on, anyway?"

"Now you know the answer to that. I'm on the horse's side, if I've gotta pick a side."

"Alright, I guess that was unfair."

Gwen was getting pressed from all sides. She wanted to

feel good about herself, but as she stared blankly at the hallway floor, she was beginning to doubt her own abilities.

"Okay, I'll call Johnny and try and persuade him to hold off a little longer, and I'll call you tomorrow."

"Sounds good. Talk to ya then."

Johnny spent the better part of the night key-whacking sentences into his word processor, only to erase most of what he entered. It was 9:30 pm when he sent his final copy to print.

From the Lexington Herald Leader 5/10/96.

In the course of reasonable endeavor and in keeping with the spirit of true journalism, every now and then the staff at the Herald Leader is confronted with a decision about certain information. Information that, when publicized, could negatively affect the outcome of an event.

I recently became aware of what appears to be a serious problem regarding the overwhelming occurrence of stillborn Thoroughbred foals. For whatever reason, healthy mares in the Central Kentucky area have been plagued with an abnormal number of stillborns. Although every effort to understand and correct the problem is being made, it appears the solution has yet to be found.

The staff at the Herald Leader does not wish to perpetuate this story further until a definitive answer or reason is determined. Names of the affected farms and infected animals shall remain confidential. It is with heart-felt regret we report this unheralded and sorrowful information. God-speed a quick and lasting turn of events.

Chapter 41

"Mr. Stone, this is Tuck Flannery."

"Now I know why you called, Mr. Flannery, but I really had no choice, I had to print something."

"No, no, I liked the way you handled it. I just wanted to thank you for the way you wrote it."

"Well thanks, I hope the rest of the horse-world thinks the way you do."

"I can't speak for any of them, but I think you did the right thing."

"What about that gal from the research center? What's she think? She never did return any of my calls and I really don't think she cares for my profession," said Johnny.

"She's never said that to me. She's been busting her butt to find what this thing's all about, so please cut her some slack."

"Well, like I said in the article, I won't print anything further until we know something positive."

"Tell you what. I'll try and do a better job of keeping you updated."

"That sounds good to me and hey, thanks again," said Johnny, as he hung up the phone.

So often, in the news business, one story doesn't satisfy the hungry minds of people who want to know what's going on in their own community, and Johnny's column seemed to unleash a collective curiosity. Following the mass of letters and phone calls they'd received from throughout the state, it wasn't long before Sam Stroub was pushing his ace reporter for a follow-up article.

"Sam, I told them we wouldn't perpetuate the story until we had the facts. Hell, I can't go back on that now."

"Hey, we don't make the world, and people have a desire and a right to know what's happening in their neck of the words. And there's nothing we can do about that, we have an obligation to let them know."

"So, whadda want me to do, pull it outta my butt?"

"Just write about the industry. You know, make it sound like it's a supporting story. I mean without all the facts."

"Oh really, mind telling me how we go about doing that?"

"Now don't tell me that mind of yours can't think up something to write about. I know better than that."

"Sure I can. But they'd see right through it."

Johnny was puzzled. He'd thought his boss was behind him in this, but realized he'd been pushing him all the way.

"I know, but at least we're buying time. I'm not saying it's got to win the Pulitzer for crissakes, just buy us some time." Sam wanted to stand behind Johnny, but he also had his finger on the pulse of the community, and knew their hunger for information. Plus, he also had a business to run.

"Okay, but you might not like it. Maybe I'll write about the average age of a horse. No, I got it. I'll write about the average weight of a stud," said Johnny, facetiously.

"No, I got an idea. Write about the average age of a reporter. That's what you need," said Sam, unable to keep from laughing, as Johnny flipped him the finger.

From the Herald Leader   5/23/96.

What happens to the racehorse when life is over? And when is it determined that the noble stallion or mare has reached the end of the stretch? Most horsemen I have interviewed, over the years, despise this subject. They usually say the decision lies solely with the owner, as it should. On the positive side we have one of the greatest racehorses in history in Bold Ruler, who, in his eighteenth year, developed cancer in his upper nasal passage and was humanely destroyed after a series of cobalt treatments could not completely cure the heralded champion. Bold Ruler did, however, live long enough to become one of the most successful breeding studs of all time, siring the immeasurable Secretariat.

But some horses are destroyed long before they have a chance to live. Horses who, for whatever reason, develop neither speed nor stamina and are nothing more to their owners than an investment liability. What becomes of them? This is the side of horse racing that is not discussed publicly. Where the operative word is Business. I have heard it said on many occasions that racehorses are not pets, and if you think of them like that, you cannot be successful. When the animal has become a red mark on the owner's expense account, it is time to cut the loss. Losses are cut every day in every business venture, but how many result in the death of a living, breathing being. In short, this is a tough business. For every Kentucky Derby entrant, there are ten thousand almost good-as horses that could have and should have been. But dreams can leave you broke in a hurry in this business.

I believe people living in the Bluegrass owe a debt of gratitude to the horse farmers who provide us this beautiful environment. And along with that must come the awesome decisions necessary to maintain that beauty. Whenever I read or hear about a horse's demise, whether an ancient warrior like Bold Ruler, a champion three-year-old like Ruffian, or a three day old foal yet unnamed, I think about a poem I once read. A poem which reminds me that Thoroughbreds are here on loan. And when they die, they return unto God.

The Thoroughbred

I'm here on loan for all the world to see,
Reflections of God's love through my beauty.

With sunlight shining on my chestnut hair,
I come and go through Heaven's stately fair.

My muscles rippling strong beneath my skin;
My eyes, majestic pools to bathe within.

And if you understood my winning need,
The thunder of my hooves and blinding speed,

Then maybe someday you will come to know,
That God could never really let me go.

I'm here on loan for all the world to see,
Reflections of His love through my beauty.

It was late in the afternoon when Tuck called Gwen to report his activity with the gathering of farm managers.

"Hey Gwen, this is Tuck. I've called the managers and they're ready to meet. What's next?"

"How about Monday morning at the research center, say about 11? Is that good for you?"

"I'll make it good for me and I'll make sure that everybody's there. Man, this thing's getting scary."

"Yeah, I know. By the way, I read Johnny's articles and we better act fast. I should be upset, but I can't do anything about it now."

"Yeah, he called me. He was concerned about how you'd take it. I guess he was up against the wall. I like what he wrote, though. I thought he showed a lot of sensitivity."

"Yeah, that's why I can't get too upset with him. Okay, I'll just see you Monday then."

Chapter 42

The warm morning breeze jostled the huge maple trees flanking the University of Kentucky campus, as the members of what would become known as the Bluegrass Coalition came together at the research center conference room. They included managers from the following establishments: Fairhaven Farm, Castlelawn Farm, where Prince of Dreams had sired six stillborns, Cherry Lane Stud and the famous Foolish Gesture, who'd sired seven stillborns, Ladymire Farm, whose heralded champion Dancing Star had sired five stillborns, Chestnut Hall Farm, Stallion Manor, where Hail My Chief stood, Shadowlyn Farm, Whirlwind Farm, Stonewyche Farm and Turbalinda Farm, where the majestic Royal Thunder, sire of nine stillborns, stood.

"Gentlemen," began Tuck. "We all know why we're here and I believe we all know Doctor Gardot. If you haven't met her personally, you've spoken with her on the phone. Doctor," Tuck nodded toward Gwen indicating she should take over.

"Yes, I believe I have spoken with everyone here. Gentlemen, I won't waste your time. I'd like for you to meet Doctor Radabaugh, director of the Livestock Disease and Diagnostic Center. Doctor Radabaugh and I, along with several of the staff, have been working day and night to solve this problem. I know you've been waiting patiently for an answer, or a cause, but, to put it bluntly," she said looking over at Dr. Radabaugh for assurance, "we simply have not found one. At this point, we know neither cause, nor solution."

With that, the room broke into questions from several of the managers. To regain order, Dr. Radabaugh quickly took the lead.

"Now don't panic, we didn't say we couldn't help. We're not sure we will ever completely solve the problem, but we believe we can contain it."

All eyes and ears were focused on Dr. Radabaugh.

"It appears that all the stillborns have been the progeny of a very select group of stallions, each of which are from one of your farms. We know, or at least we think we know, exactly which stallions have been infected. With that information we believe we can contain this virus, and I am calling it a virus because, at this time, we don't have a name for it."

"What do you mean, contain it?" asked one of the managers, known for neither his patience nor his tact.

"Good question. In simple terms, gentlemen, we plan to quarantine all infected animals. I have a list of what we believe to be the infected stallions. We must find all mares covered, or in foal to these studs and quarantine them. I'm not completely sure, but I don't believe we have any live, infected offspring at this time. At least none that we know of. Does anyone dispute that?"

Following a long moment of silence, Dr. Radabaugh asked, "Does anyone know of any other farm experiencing this problem? I mean outside of those represented here today?"

Without receiving a positive response, Dr. Radabaugh passed out a list of infected stallions to all farm managers. It read like a Thoroughbred who's who, including: Heart Lancer, Prince of Dreams, Foolish Gesture, Dancing Star, Loquation, Hail My Chief, Fire to Thee, Royal Thunder, Flight Whisper and Chatogyn.

As the members of the Coalition read the list, a shroud of silence overcame the group, as each participant saw the name of his prized stallion prancing off the page.

"What now?" asked Tuck "I mean, we turn them out, but what about the mares in foal?"

"They must also be quarantined. What happens to the foals is up to you," said Dr. Radabaugh.

"Well, what choice do we have?" said Tuck. "I mean, you know this business. If there's no cure, we have no choice. We've got to do what's right."

"Hey, that's up to the owners, hell, I'm not gonna make

that call," said one of the managers, angrily.

"And they'll want to know when this thing is gonna be cured. What do I tell them?"

"We cannot promise a cure," said Dr. Radabaugh. "We are doing everything we can, but we may not find the cure for quite some time. I can tell you that we have never seen anything like this before. Not in the annals of our collective research."

The members of the Coalition didn't expect such negative news. Nervously they avoided looking directly at each other.

"We've got to contact the owners of these horses. Not only the foals, but the mares and stallions," said Tuck. "They'll have to make the decision. They own the animals, not us."

"Doctor Gardot and I will be available to all of you anytime, and I can assure you we will do everything in our power to save these animals," said Dr. Radabaugh.

"Now, think about how many mares have been covered, and when did it all start? You will have to research your stud's activities back as far as the beginning of last year. All the way from January. All offspring, whether healthy or not, must be quarantined," said Dr. Radabaugh.

"We will need to examine all the foals that have survived, as well as all, and I mean ALL," Dr. Radabaugh looked at each manager as he spoke, "associated mares. And don't forget to quarantine the mares still in foal. The stallions must be stopped immediately. No more breeding to the studs on this list. Are we together on this?"

Each member of the Coalition nodded approval, as Tuck said, "Well, I guess we've got our work cut out for us."

"Can we all meet back here again in a few days?" asked Gwen. "I'd like to think we can come together as a team."

The members agreed that, after discussing the situation with their respective owners, they would meet at the research center within five days to formulate an isolation plan. No one was interested in discussing the options further. No one had the stomach. Not for now, at least.

Chapter 43

Kalea Jackson, a first year graduate student at the University of Kentucky, and writer for the Bittervetch, a semi-underground newspaper, was finishing her bagel and coffee at the Student Union Building, when her eye caught the article on the back page of the Herald Leader. She was planning to remain on campus for the summer, but was preparing to head home for the weekend when she became curious about the article she'd just finished. Always on the lookout for interesting information, something about the article she was reading registered with her.

Stillborns, she thought. *In the Bluegrass? Something about this just isn't right. And what's this mean "the outcome of the event." What's the event?*

She thought about calling Johnny Stone, or possibly going over to his office for an interview, but didn't want to appear overly aggressive which might earn her a negative reputation. She knew she might want to work there someday. After thinking it through, she decided to wait and see how things developed, but she couldn't get the thought of stillborn horses out of her mind.

Why are they writing about an infection and then less than two weeks later, they're writing about destroying horses?

Her curiosity had been piqued with Johnny's initial stillborn article, but now she suspected something strange was going on and she wanted to get to the bottom of it.

Are they going to destroy some of the infected horses? How would anyone know? Are they concerned at all about the animals?

Her mind filled with questions, while driving the 85 miles to Louisville where her family lived.

Daddy would know, she thought, entering I-64 westbound.

Wilbur "Slab" Jackson and his wife Hattie, decided early

on in their marriage that they would see to it that all their children received a college education, and when Kalea came along, the summer of 1974, she would be the last. They lived a modest life owning a small home in East Louisville, not far from where Mohammad Ali was born and raised.

"I knew that boy was gonna make it," Kalea often heard her daddy say. "When he was a boy, he'd never sit still. Run everywhere. Never sit still. Always running and doing. Skinny kid, but good looking. Good kid too, never no lip. Funny, how he got being called the Lip. The Louisville Lip, ha." Wilbur'd say.

Wilbur loved Churchill Downs and, whenever the horses were running, you could bet he'd find any and every excuse to be there. He loved everything about the track, the smell, the flowers, the people, the money, but most of all, the horses.

"Daddy, did you see those articles in the Herald Leader the last few weeks? One about stillborns? And then the one about how and when to put horses down?"

"Can't say as I did," he said, as they sat around the kitchen table eating pieces of Hattie's cherry pie and whipped cream. "What about it, baby?"

If Wilbur had a weakness other than his love for the track, it was a hopeless adoration for his daughters, especially his pride and joy, Kalea.

"It just hit me wrong. I mean first of all, the paper doesn't want to write details about this infection, or whatever it is they're experiencing. Then they write something about when to destroy a horse. It seems to me the equine industry is getting ready to do something, but the news media doesn't know how to write about it. My guess is, they're about to destroy some horses."

"No kiddin'. How many?" asked Hattie.

"They didn't say. All they said was they were sorry it happened and until they get all the facts, they weren't gonna print it. Seems crazy to me."

"Tell ya what, baby. Me and you'll go't the track and see if we can't smell something out. How's that?", winking at Kalea.

"Works for me."

Kalea felt the tender love that only her mother's cooking and her daddy's kindly gaze could provide.

It was a humid, rainy day, as Kalea and her daddy walked between the barns on the Backside of Churchill Downs. Although there were not many people out and about, there was an older gentleman there by the name of Woody "Third Shoe" Scalhone, who'd gotten his name from the days when he could tap dance so well folks claimed he had a third foot. Woody had been just about every kind of horseman in his seventy-one years, and Wilbur knew him well.

"What about it?" asked Wilbur, as he and Kalea walked into the back of barn 16.

"Well I'll be a," said Woody, sticking out his hand for Wilbur to shake. "Ain't seen you in no telling how damn long. What brings you back out this way?"

"Oh, just trying to keep my hand from getting cold, you know how it is. This here's my daughter Kalea. Honey, say hello to the oldest man in the world."

"Now watch yoself, I can still get up on the flo and that's a fact."

"Yeah, I betcha can. Hell, Woody used to dance for all of us when we was kids."

"Now boy, dontcha be telling no lies now. I bet I ain't got five years on you no how."

"Say Woody, been hearing 'bout some outbreak of some disease over 'round Lexington at some a them big farms. You heard anything like that?"

With his facial expression changing from grin to frown, Woody quickly looked down at the straw on the brick floor. "Yeah, but I don't know 'bout no disease. Mostly stillborns. Rumor is, they gonna put down some mares, maybe even some stallions, if they ain't already. Don't know what's got 'em, but they ain't gonna fool 'round with it. They just gonna down 'em."

"I knew it," said Kalea. "They've been printing stories like they were gonna do something like that. Hinting at it anyway."

"Well, that's just the way it is, sad to say," said Woody. "I hates to see it, but that's just the way it is."

At one time Woody worked for the now defunct Halley-Bright stables, travelling to all the well known tracks, grooming some of the finest horses of his day. Always a softy when it came to the horses, he would cringe whenever he heard of a mishap or an accident. It was his greatest misfortune in life, however, to be in just the wrong place at just the wrong time that July afternoon in 1975.

"Yeah, I sure am glad I ain't 'round any of that. I've had enough of it. Can't stand to see what they hafta do, sometimes."

Not understanding what Woody was referring to, Kalea asked, "What do you mean?"

"Just that I was there when they had to put down the greatest hoss I ever saw. You remember that?" pointing to Wilbur. "You remember who's the greatest hoss you ever saw?"

"You mean that filly?" asked Wilbur.

"You damn right. Best I ever saw. And I had to watch her go down. Broke my heart too."

"Who was that?" asked Kalea.

"She was a big, huge, almost black filly named Ruffian. Huge hoss. Every time she stepped on the track and I mean EVERY time she went out, she broke a record. Ain't no hoss ever done that. Won every race she ever ran. Couldn't be beat. She just ran right out of her shoes. And that's what got her. She was just too big for her own shoes."

"Aw, she was something now," echoed Wilbur.

"She musta weighed 1300 pounds or so, but her hooves were just too small to carry it. Anyway, she was matched against the Derby winner that year. Let's see now, 1975. Foolish Pleasure. Good hoss too. I was up in New York at the time. Belmont Park. Every eye was on those two. Loaded 'em side by side way out on the second turn. Mile and a quarter I think. Anyhow, they broke out the gate and run about a quarter mile neck and neck. And just when the filly was pulling away, CRACK. She broke down. Wouldn't stop though, just kept running. She wouldn't let that colt get by her. Never let any hoss get by her.

Gazing off into the distance, like he was seeing it all over again in his mind, Woody stopped talking. Kalea and Wilbur could tell the old man was moved.

"By the time that jock got her stopped, her hoof was dangling by some skin and tendons, and blood was gushing out her leg, man just about the worst thing I ever did see. Every one of us rushed to help her. Wish I didn't go, man, I just wish'd I'd never seen it. But did she ever have heart. Just too much heart."

With a sadness in his eyes Wilbur'd never seen before the old tap dancer said, "Had to put her down that night. Can't nobody understand she was the greatest hoss I ever saw. How can they, she died before she could prove me right. But she's the best I ever saw."

"A filly," said Kalea, softly.

"Yes ma'am, a filly. Don't matter what she was, she was the best."

"Sure wish I'd seen her," said Kalea.

"There's a picture of her in the office. Don't know who wrote that poem 'bout her, but sho' is nice. Brings me to tears every time I reads it."

Wilbur and Kalea walked over to the office and found the picture of Ruffian on the wall. "Read it to me, baby," said Wilbur.

Ruffian

To watch you streaming down the stretch, your colors on display.
To smash another record or just chase the wind away.
Was nothing shy of perfect as you sailed upon the breeze.
Holding every heartbeat, while running with such ease.

From Claiborne Farm where you were born to Carolina you would go.
To learn your role of champion, the greatest I would know.
You never came in second, and to show was not your style.
From Spring to Fall you won them all, faster every mile.

Then you and Foolish Pleasure were loaded side by side.
To race the Derby winner on your famous final ride.
As you began to take the lead, you heard that fateful sound.
The bone in your right foreleg snapped - you had broken down.

A nation stood in silence as they took you out the back.
No one moved and nothing soothed the hurt felt round that track.
I went to bed with hope that you would race another day.
And yet I knew deep down inside, it wouldn't be that way.

Then Heaven's homeward angel, gave your spirit flight.
As mortal fans we woke to find you taken in the night.
But I cannot forget you as through my mind you roam.
To graze my memory's pastures and call my heart your home.

Now records left unbroken, and foals you never had.
Plague my conscience now and then and make the moment sad.
Though maybe down His backstretch, I'll see you run again
But here on earth, I'll wonder first - what you might have been.

Chapter 44

Returning to Lexington Kalea contemplated how she would write the story describing the destruction of helpless animals. She even thought about organizing a protest of sorts, but didn't know exactly how to go about it. Enlisting a friend to help her who, in turn, brought a friend who knew a friend, before she realized what was happening, she'd amassed a small army of interested students young and old alike, willing to aid in her cause. They'd printed and distributed flyers around the university campus and the adjoining neighborhoods, and had published several articles in the Bittervetch. Among them, one which started...

Should Horses Die For Profit?

What society would permit the destruction of a live being solely for profit? Are there no rights for animals in the state of Kentucky? It appears, sadly enough, that there are not.

They'd set up tables near the Student Union Building to solicit signatures. Not completely sure where they were heading, they hoped they could positively affect the senseless destruction of horses. But it was Kalea's dedication and passionate statements during a live interview with a local TV station that caught future state representative, Fran Filburn's eye.

Looking for an elective edge and a reason to increase her local popularity, Filburn decided to jump on the bandwagon taking up Kalea's cause. Gaining several hundred signatures herself, Filburn challenged the state legislature to take a stand on what she claimed to be the needless destruction of animals.

With political pressure mounting from all sides, and not wanting additional negative press, several members of the Bluegrass Coalition along with Dr. Radabaugh, decided to disclose to the public the problems they were facing. Formulating a plan to maintain the health and well-being of all infected animals, they met with Fran Filburn and Kalea Jackson to disclose their plan. following a lengthy meeting at the research center, Gwen Gardot called Johnny Stone in an effort to quell the disturbing dilemma.

"Mr. Stone, this is Doctor Gardot."

"Well now, it sure is good to hear from you. I guess things are getting a bit out of hand, hey?"

"Can we meet tomorrow? I'd like to talk to you about making a statement."

"Well, I don't see why not. Just tell me where and when. I think we should include that journalism student over at UK. She's been hounding me for information. Might as well bring her in up front."

"Don't worry about her. She's already up to speed on what's happening."

"Okay, I'll see you tomorrow."

The following afternoon Gwen met with Johnny and Kalea to inform them that the horse owners and farm managers had come to a decision. With a concerned look on her tired face, she opened the conversation.

"They promised they wouldn't put the stallions or the mares down."

"Does that mean under any circumstances?" asked Johnny.

"They assured me that all affected horses will be allowed to live out their natural lives. The Governor has stated that he would see to it that the mares are kept at the Kentucky Horse Park, provided the owners don't want them. The stallions will remain at each of the farms where they now stand, unless the Horse Park wants them. All horses will be sterilized, but none will be put down."

"Hallelujah," cried Johnny. "That's the best news I've

heard all year. But, do you think this will be enough to contain the disease?"

"I sure hope so. We'll continue our research, you can bet on that."

"You mean, that you haven't found a cure for this?" asked Kalea.

"No, but we think we have a solution. It's just that it's not really a cure. Not at this point. We just haven't been able to isolate the cause."

"So, the mares will remain in quarantine at the Horse Park?"

"Yes, for awhile, but it shouldn't be for long. I don't believe they are contagious in any way, but we're going to keep a close eye on them."

"Hell Doc, that may become a tourist attraction," said Johnny, quickly realizing it wasn't that funny.

"Yeah, I know, but I don't think that's the way we want to showcase Kentucky."

"Are there any other facilities looking into this?" asked Kalea.

"We've brought in the finest minds in the equine world and have sent samples to several labs for identification, but so far we've just not been able to draw any conclusions," said Gwen.

"So, I can put that in my article?" asked Johnny.

"I don't think so. We probably shouldn't give out all the details as yet. You never know what might happen."

"What do you mean, Doc?"

"I just don't think the populace needs to know all the details. I mean we really don't know what it is we're working with yet. No sense to say anything we might regret later."

"Or have to defend," said Kalea. "Right Doctor?"

Gwen glanced at Kalea with a blank look on her face.

"Okay, I'll get this out tonight," said Johnny. "And don't worry Doc, I know what to print."

Gwen looked at Johnny for a long moment before saying,

"Look, Mr. Stone. I know I was kind of rough on you. I'm sorry for some of the things I've said."

"Aw, you don't owe me an apology. I know how bad this must be on you, Doc and please, call me Johnny."

"Okay, thanks Johnny."

"Thank you Doctor," said Kalea, walking out the door with Johnny.

Gwen drove home thinking she'd done everything in her power to solve the problems at hand, realizing she was no closer to a solution than when she'd started. Life used to be good, especially living in the Bluegrass, but things were just not the same. She knew the malady would be extremely hard to uncover, and she wondered if a cure would ever be found.

Johnny went straight to work writing the most important article of his career. It read...

> I was hoping against all odds that the recent Thoroughbred stillborn episodes would conclude in a positive manner. Nonetheless, I felt it my duty to prepare the reader for a negative ending, not the least of which could have been the destruction of some of Kentucky's more prized stallions and mares.
>
> It gives me the utmost satisfaction to report that there will be NO untimely death of a Thoroughbred whose misfortune has been to become involved with this dreaded and unknown disease. During a recent meeting held by representatives of the owners of the infected animals, it was decided that the infected mares and stallions will be allowed to live until natural death, at either the farm on which they now stand, or stabled at the Kentucky Horse Park.
>
> It is, however, a shame that all of the affected offspring were either stillborn or euthanized shortly after birth, due to unrecoverable circumstances.

The Kentucky Equine Research Center has vowed to continue researching the cause of this catastrophic disease, and plans to study the infected horses over the next several months.

The sun dropped beneath the horizon bringing closure to another torrid day in the Bluegrass, as a small black bag containing a deadly device programed to explode when the atmospheric pressure dropped below a certain threshold, sat in the corner of a priest's closet in northern Philadelphia. A certain threshold found somewhere around 12,000 feet above sea level.

Chapter 45

After pondering how he was going to regain her good graces, Rajad sent Darkside to Jules' apartment with four dozen roses, and an invitation for her to dine with him at the royal palace.

"He is very, very sorry madam and wishes you would accept these flowers as a symbol of his affection. He also wishes you would consider dining with him at your earliest convenience."

Jules knew this was Rajad's way of making up with her, but she also knew it was the perfect opportunity for her to enact her revenge. After all, he did slap her around and would continue abusing her, if something or someone didn't stop him. Someone with just the right talent, knowledge, and deviant nature to do so.

"Please tell Prince Rajad that I will be available to dine with him next Thursday."

"As you wish madam."

This gave Jules ample time to decide what to do. She knew she was capable of perfecting a genetic poison to rid the planet of certain breeds of animals, could she now develop a simple concoction to rid the earth of one diabolical prince? She plotted her method while making her way to her laboratory. A place of solace, a place of meditation, and a place of murder.

Walking into the palace as though she owned it, Jules wore a black, low cut, full-length evening gown and four-inch heels. Approaching Rajad, she allowed him to kiss her hand, but resisted his attempts at getting closer. There was a different look in her eyes than he'd seen before, causing his cat-like sense of danger to stir.

"Jules, you look absolutely stunning."

"So, what's for dinner?" she asked, nonchalantly.

"Please, please, come have some champagne. We must

celebrate our, shall we say, rekindling."

Knowing how cunning Rajad could be, she tried throwing him off guard, placing him on the defensive. "Hold your horses," she said, with a smile. "You've been pretty damn mean to me."

"Please, my love, please. Let us not talk of that. Not tonight anyway. Allow the bad fruits of that night to spoil forever."

"I didn't know you were a poet," she said, cutting the tension.

Allowing him to think her feelings were softening, the evening progressed cagingly, until they were interrupted by one of Rajad's servants, who bowed to whisper in his ear.

"Would you excuse me, please?" he asked, as he left the room.

Seizing the moment, Jules reached beneath her skirt unleashing a small packet she'd attached to the elastic of one of her nylons. Nervously, she opened the container, running her finger along the jelly-like substance adhered to the wall of the wrapper, like glue. Smearing a portion of the gel inside Rajad's glass, she looked around before filling it with champagne. As the prince returned, she held up her glass proposing a toast.

"Salud, my Prince."

Lifting his glass in return, Rajad responded... "And to us, my dear. And to us."

She was not one of God's chosen few, and her name would never be heard echoing through the halls of sanctum, but one could rest assured that Jules Weherner could concoct a darn good poison. Whether it be a substance affecting the lineage of horses, or one's own circulation, she was, without doubt, in a class by herself.

It took less than an hour for Rajad's vital organs to begin shutting down, about the time Jules arrived back at her own apartment. He'd wanted to spend the night with her, but with her claim of a headache she managed, successfully, to thwart his advances.

Changing into his nightshirt, Rajad felt warm blood trickling from his nose. Entering his ornate bathroom, he experienced a tightness above his stomach coupled with the distinct feeling that he couldn't breathe. Beginning to wheeze, he glared frantically into the gigantic mirror in search of an answer, but to no avail. With the abnormalities of his collective sensations, he stumbled from the bathroom to the bedroom to summon his man-servant, but discovered, to his horror, that no vocal sound accompanied his call. He tried to run, but instead fell to the floor in excruciating pain, flailing his arms and legs furiously in a futile, panic-stricken attempt to breathe. It was over in minutes, as he slowly suffocated within the walls of the sanctuary that had protected him for the greater part of his life.

The morning sun crept stealthily along the barren desert dunes, as rigor mortis crept through the inroads of Rajad's crumpled body. It was determined, officially, that the prince had sustained a heart attack, possibly due to stress, overwork, or the loss of his father. For the second time in less than six months, Karoumi was thrown into royal mourning.

Chapter 46

"Your breakfast is ready Father, now don't let your eggs get cold, come and eat," said Mrs. Maloney, the 68 year old attendant who cooked and cleaned for the priests at St. Stephen's Catholic Church in northern Philadelphia.

"Thank you dear," said Father Petrie in his characteristically soft voice, even though he hadn't been himself since Monsignor McSourley had passed away. Not only had he handled all the funeral arrangements and the Requiem High Mass, he also hosted and cared for the Monsignor's family as well as for Bishop Dunn.

"Mrs. Maloney, would you call Trans Atlantic and arrange for that black bag to be sent to its rightful owner? It must have been switched when I had to cancel my flight last December. Can't imagine what happened to mine."

Having been used for carrying gifts to his old friends living in Europe, it had taken Father Petrie several months before realizing one of the bags he'd brought home from the airport was not his at all. It belonged, according to the name on the small plastic card attached to the handle, to Mrs. Dimitri L. Lugossi of Rome, Italy.

"Of course Father, I'll call them straight away."

"What would I ever do without you, dear?"

"Starve, most likely Father," she chuckled.

The black bag was picked up at the rectory by an airport representative, delivered to Trans Atlantic's baggage claim office at Kennedy Airport, and found its way aboard the evening flight to Rome. Inside the bag was a new-age explosive device developed by a disgruntled Union Carbide chemical engineer who marketed his invention to Iraq and other terrorist countries. The explosive power of the bomb was astronomical given its small size and disguisable capabilities, rendering it impossible, without hands-on inspection, to be detected by the electronic surveillance system at JFK.

Having devised a plan to rid himself of his brother once and for all, Prince Rajad procured the device through his illicit, underground channels. Knowing Efram would be returning to Karoumi aboard the Trans Atlantic flight the evening of December 21st, he'd ordered the bomb planted in the baggage compartment at JFK.

Regardless how tight the security, it never fails to amaze even the staunchest NTSB officials what money and power can accomplish. Among the many theories offered by both NTSB and FBI participants, was a missile fired from off-shore, defective wiring, an act of God and finally a bomb, possibly sabotage. But sadly enough, in the final analysis, what actually caused the Boeing 747 jumbo jet to explode, shortly after the controller at Boston's Air Route Traffic Control Center had directed the pilot to begin climbing to an altitude of 15,000 feet, was never proven.

It may well have been merely an accident that the black bags were mistakenly switched, but those unfortunate souls who boarded Trans Atlantic's Flight 718 that fateful night, probably never knew what hit them. At just over 1,4000 feet the bomb exploded in the cargo hold, tearing the plane in half where the wings join the fuselage. The wings and aft section of the plane continued in an upward direction for several moments before spiraling into the ocean, while the cabin and fuselage ahead of the wings plunged immediately downward. Many speculate that the gargantuan rush of air most likely knocked everyone in the aft section unconscious immediately following the explosion, while those in the front of the plane watched in horror, as they fell helplessly into the unmerciful waves.

"Have you seen the paper this morning, Father? Isn't it awful, over two hundred people and not far from here too," said Mrs. Maloney, as she handed him the newspaper while placing his coffee on the table in front of him.

"Dear Mother of God. I was scheduled on that flight only a

few months ago."

Finishing his coffee and deciding against breakfast, he excused himself and walked slowly into his study to kneel beside the small alter he kept for prayer. Placing his fingers on his rosary he began the first Hail Mary, his eyes filling with tears and his mind fading to thoughts of his brother Thomas, who died aboard Air West's Flight 972 over the South Pacific, eight years earlier. He'd accepted Thomas' death as he was trained to do, but didn't understand how tragedies like this kept happening.

When will it ever stop.

Chapter 47

Meredith couldn't believe her ears when she'd heard that Prince Rajad was dead. Thinking about what she'd overheard in the lab bathroom, she couldn't help but think that Jules had something to do with it.

"She's involved, Bill. I just know it."

"Now, we don't know that," said Bill not believing his own words. "I mean, we don't have any evidence."

"Evidence! What do you call him slapping her around? What about killing that man they argued about, or whatever it was?"

"I know, I know."

What are we going to do?" asked Meredith.

"We need to confront her, but we have to be careful here. She may be dangerous."

"I know, but we just can't let this go without doing something. What will we say to her? Hi, how ya been? Did you kill the prince?"

Even though the situation wasn't funny, the statement brought a smile to Bill's face.

"Well we've got to do something. What if I confronted her?" asked Bill.

"No, we both should do it. We both know what's going on."

"We do? How do you get that? I sure as hell don't know what's going on."

"You know what I mean," said Meredith, not wanting to smile.

The next afternoon, they waited in Meredith's office for Jules to arrive.

"Does she suspect? What did you say to get her to come up?"

"I just called down and asked if she could meet me in my

office at two o'clock. I don't think she suspects. But, she must be in an awful frame of mind. Oh, here she is now. Come in," said Meredith, noticing Jules approaching.

Jules' eyes shifted quickly between Bill and Meredith, as she entered the office.

"Hello people. How are you?"

"Fine," said Meredith.

"Great," said Bill, walking over and giving Jules a hug. "You're looking good."

"Thanks, but I'm not feeling so good. Just can't believe all the tragedy these past few months."

"Yes," said Meredith. "I was thinking the same thing."

"Tell me, Jules. Weren't you and the prince sort of seeing each other?" asked Bill.

Jules' eyes widened, as she went immediately on the defensive.

"Well, no, not really. I mean we were just sort of, well friends. I mean we had a few drinks together, but we weren't seeing each other."

"There's a rumor going around, Jules, that you were the last one to see the prince. I mean alive."

"Well, that's just not true. Who would start a rumor like that?" Jules was getting angry.

"Jules," said Meredith. "Please understand that we're your friends. Is there anything you want to tell us?"

"Friends? Is this how you treat your friends? What do you want me to say. What are you, some kind of lynch mob?"

Meredith crossed the room to give Jules a hug, but Jules shoved her away saying, "Leave me alone. What right do you have to question me?"

"Please Jules," begged Bill. "we're on your side."

Jules looked at Bill and then Meredith and then back at Bill, with a sneer on her face before saying. "Stay away from me, I'm warning you."

With that, Jules turned and ran out slamming the door behind her.

"Well, that was pleasant," said Bill. "Maybe we should invite her out for drinks next time."

"I surely didn't expect she'd act like that," said Meredith. "So, what do we do now?"

"Didn't she say something about infecting some horses? And wasn't it back in Kentucky? Maybe we should make a few phone calls and see if anything's going on."

"I'll call in the morning. Right now I don't feel so good."

In her quest for power, Jules had turned her evil attention to Karoumi's newest sheikh, plotting her next affair and a more palatial position, envisioning herself sharing the throne, as Karoumi's Queen of State. Oblivious of her treacherous plan, Efram remained engulfed in mourning, opening the last of the many condolence letters, when one in particular caught his eye. It read...

My Dearest Sheikh,

I was so deeply saddened by the untimely death of your brother so soon after the death of your beloved father. I know that you believe that Allah is always with you and, to a much meeker extent, so am I.

I have experienced a loss such as yours in my life and I fully understand your pain and sorrow. Please remember that you remain in my prayers and in my heart.

Sincerely,

Jules Werhner

Chapter 48

Efram felt the weight of the world on his shoulders, having buried, within months, the two remaining members of his immediate family. From early childhood he wanted more than anything to follow in his father's footsteps and lead his country into a new and enlightened future, but nothing had prepared him for the depression he now felt. He prayed constantly to have his burdens of guilt and loneliness reduced but could not seem to find peace of mind. Not, that is, until he read Jules Werhner's note. It was sad that such an intelligent person could find comfort from such a worthless source.

She'd done what no other person on earth had been able to do, being in the perfect place at the perfect time, and she was betting that Efram's sorrow and distraction could provide the timely platform from which to spring a trap. A trap that could provide her a lucrative and secure future.

It was hardly a month following Rajad's death, that she began to plot and plan her role as Queen of Karoumi. How she could save face and remain on Meredith's staff while gaining Efram's favors was on her mind, while planning her visit with the Sheikh of Karoumi. It was unfortunate for her that she was preceded on Efram's royal list of friends by none other than Karoumi's own handsome ambassador.

Darkside had always felt that Efram was a much better prince than Rajad, but didn't have a chance to serve the older brother, until now. Understanding, full well, the young sheikh's sadness, Darkside approached Efram in a respectful manner and, before the sheikh could prevent him, fell to his knees pledging his undying loyalty.

"Please, my son do not prostrate before me. You are a noble subject and a loyal friend. You have cared well for my brother and in doing so, have also cared for me."

Darkside softly spoke. "My life is your life, my Sheikh. I live only to serve you. I will serve and protect you as you have served and protected us for so very long."

Efram had no idea that Darkside's protection would begin immediately. Darkside knew that Rajad and Jules had plotted, not only to destroy the Thoroughbred industry, but to kill Efram as well. And he knew that Rajad's death had most likely been at the hands of Jules. He realized and was at peace in the knowledge, that he was now serving a leader worthy of his loyalty. It was just after dark when Jules heard the knock on her apartment door.

"Yes?" said Jules, recognizing the dark eyed man who'd brought her flowers once before.

"Excuse me madam, may I have a word with you?" asked Darkside.

"Well, I guess so. Sure come on in. What can I do for you?"

"I think, madam, that it would be best if you now were to return to the United States."

"What? Why, what's going on?" demanded Jules, her lioness' instincts awakening to the ominous tone in Darkside's voice.

"I believe my country would be better off if you would return to the United States," said Darkside, more sternly.

"Now just a damn minute. Who the hell do you think you're talking to. Do you know who I am?"

Darkside snapped his fingers and two of his accomplices appeared at the apartment door.

"What is this?"

Darkside could be very kind when he wanted to be, but when he wanted to scare the hell out of a young woman alone and far from home, he could be unbelievably hostile. Staring at her and approaching her until his face was an inch away from hers, he said very deliberately.

"Unless you would rather go home in a box, you will pack

your belongings immediately."

Scared beyond belief, Jules spent the next half hour hastily packing the suitcases she'd brought with her to Karoumi. Darkside then escorted her to the local airstrip and the waiting Lear Jet. In less than 30 minutes Jules found herself at the Dubai International Airport awaiting Trans Atlantic's New York flight. Before boarding the plane, she was forced to sign a letter addressed to Meredith informing her that she was leaving the country and would not be back. In the letter she thanked Meredith and Bill for everything they'd done for her, and told them she would write them when her life was on a more even keel.

The following morning, Meredith found the letter which had been mysteriously placed on her office desk.

"Bill, can you come up here? I found a letter on my desk this morning. It's from Jules."

"A letter? Be right there."

"So, what do you think?" she asked after Bill had read the letter.

"Your guess is as good as mine. She did the right thing, though. She was in way over her head and she knew it. I wouldn't be surprised if she didn't have something to do with the prince's death."

"This is wrong, Bill. I mean very, very wrong."

"Now I'm really confused. I mean why on earth would she leave like this?"

"There's more."

"What do you mean?"

"I made some phone calls last night. It seems that they're experiencing a big problem in Kentucky. An epidemic of stillborn foals this year. Hundreds dying in the last days before birth."

"Have they found what's causing it? I mean did they mention a cure?"

"Bill, they way Doctor Radabaugh talked, they don't have a clue."

"You're kidding. How long has it been going on?"

"Since March or so. At least that's what I was able to gather. He seemed reluctant to talk about it."

"I can't blame him. That's a pretty prestigious place. But we've got a clue, and she just left town. We've got to get to Jules. I'll bet she knows what's going on."

"What makes you think she's going to say anything? I mean she didn't talk to us when she had the chance. And we're her friends."

"I know. I know. Mere, we've got to go home. We've got to find Jules. She has to come clean."

"I know. And I'll bet she's got something to do with the problems they're having in Kentucky. I'm going to look through her lab. There's got to be some clue somewhere."

Chapter 49

Gwen thought about the events of the past few months, as she sat, pensively, in her office. It was late, and the thought of calling Tuck crossed her mind, but she didn't want to appear pushy. She liked him and wished he'd called her, but was glad he hadn't due to the fact that she didn't have time for anything other than her work.

Not right now at least. Maybe when this thing's over and we all get back to normal. He's not involved with anyone and neither am I. Why couldn't it work? Maybe I'll hear from him tomorrow, she thought, locking her office and heading for the parking lot.

Johnny Stone never could forget the manner in which Jefferson Fairchild was killed. *Five bullets and all in the heart* he thought, dialing Tuck's office.

"Mr. Flannery, by any chance did you know Jefferson Fairchild?"

"Yeah, sort of. Didn't know him well though. Mostly knew of him."

"Any idea as to why he was murdered?"

"Not really. He wasn't a bad guy, but he sort of had a reputation. I liked him though, what little I knew of him."

"Did you know he was found with five bullets in his heart."

"I didn't know that. Does sound a bit strange, now that you mention it."

"I'm reaching for the sky here, but I think he might have had something to do with these stillborns."

"No kidding? How do ya figure that?"

"I don't know. Just a hunch. He was killed Mafia style. Five bullets in the heart. I don't know, but something just doesn't seem right. I mean, what would get a nobody like him killed like that?"

"Jeez, I've never thought about it. Didn't really know how he was killed. Guess I've been too busy around here to keep up with things."

"Well, keep it in the back of your mind and if anything surfaces, call me will ya?"

"Tell ya what. Let me make a few phone calls and ask around and I'll get back with ya."

"Okay, thanks."

"You bet."

That afternoon, Johnny drove out to Jefferson Fairchild's farm only to find that it was to be auctioned off the following month. Squinting to read the sign posted on the front of the property, a large white Lincoln pulled into the driveway.

"Interested?" asked the portly real-estate agent, opening the door.

"Don't know. What can you tell me about it?" asked Johnny.

"Everything, the entire property, including farm implements, tools, furniture, house and grounds is for sale. If it doesn't sell inside a month, it'll go up on auction.

"No, I mean do you know anything about the tenants?"

"To tell you the truth, the previous owner was shot to death in that house right there."

"That's what I've heard. Any idea why?"

"No sir. But I think that's why we've not had a bid on the place."

"So, he lived here alone? No family, kids?"

"Not really. Heard he had somebody living out back, though. Over there by the barn, in that shed."

"Who was that?"

"Don't know, but whoever it was, took off after the murder."

"Oh?"

"Yep, all I know is that he was gone by the time the police showed up. Least ways, that's the scuttle-butt."

"Well look, thanks for your help," said Johnny.

Chapter 50

Bill and Meredith asked for immediate leave, and flew to New York, where they decided to split up, he going to Virginia to ask Lauren for a divorce, and she to Lexington and the Kentucky Equine Research Center.

After two grueling days away from each other, Bill phoned Meredith late in the evening.

"So, how're things going?" he asked.

"Not so good. They really are having quite a problem with stillborns, and they don't have a clue what's causing it. I can't believe so many dead foals in one season. It's just heartbreaking, Bill."

"Did you mention anything about Jules?"

"I told Doctor Radabaugh what we know about her, but he seems bewildered. I really don't think he believes one person could be the cause of all of this."

"It wasn't just her. This was a conspiracy. Sure wish we knew how many people were involved. I mean Jules and the prince, but who else?"

"I know, but we can't prove anything with what little we know. Not without Jules."

"I'm going to drive over to her home tomorrow and confront her face to face. She has to come clean, that's all there is to it."

"Absolutely! There's no way she gets away with this. I don't know about you Bill, but I feel pretty bad about this. I mean aren't we somewhat responsible?"

"Now don't get me thinking along those lines. I mean, we didn't poison any horses."

"You're right. We would never do that. I'd die first and so would you. Okay, sorry I mentioned it, but we've got to make sure Jules tells the truth.

"We will, sweetheart. We will."

There was a long pause before Bill asked "What are they doing about the stillborns?"

"They've got just about everybody working on it plus they've quarantined a group of horses. There's quite a stink, I mean there's been a student protest, and a campaign to save the infected horses. Even the Governor has gotten involved."

"Sounds pretty ugly."

"It is. But, they've at least decided not to put any animals down. I do know that, and that alone makes me feel really good about the whole ordeal. So I'm not feeling as bad as I did when I got here."

"Well, that's a relief, anyway."

How's it going there? Did you talk to your wife?"

"Yeah, and she's pretty amiable. I think there may be another man in her life. Don't want to know about it, but I just have that feeling."

"Well, there's another woman in your life. Isn't there?"

"You bet there is. And boy, do I miss you."

"I miss you too, honey. I really do. When will you be here?"

"Don't know, probably by the weekend, but I just don't know yet. I've got to get some papers together and see a lawyer. I should know more within the next couple of days."

"Just remember, I love you, Bill. And take care of yourself. Will you do that for me?"

"Yes dear, you know me. I'll be okay. You take care too and remember that I love you. Will ya do that for me?"

"I love you, Bill. Bye honey."

Chapter 51

Tuck's mind went into high gear following his conversation with Johnny. Something about Jefferson Fairchild and his murder struck a chord with him. It was late in the afternoon that he hit pay-dirt, when Jimmy, the manager of Turbalinda Farm, returned his phone call.

"Hey Tuck, I think we've stumbled on to something. One of my grooms said he remembered seeing a guy he knew around the stallion barn sometime last year during the height of breeding season. He thought it was strange at the time, but he felt the guy was just looking for work. Didn't realize that Royal Thunder was in the same barn the night he saw this guy."

"Hey, Royal Thunder was one of the infected stallions."

"Yeah, and get this. This dude lived at Fairchilds' farm?"

"Are you serious?"

"Yup, and I'll bet anything this guy knows something. Why else would he disappear after Fairchild got shot?"

"We've gotta find him. Did your groom know his name?"

"Franke something. Said he didn't know him very well. Said that he was kind of a loser."

"Do you think he could find him?"

"Let me see what I can do. There's not too many places he can hide around here. If he's in the Bluegrass, we'll find him."

"Thanks Jimmy," said Tuck, hanging up the phone.

~

It didn't take Jules long to find her way back to her old stomping grounds and one of the seediest bar rooms near her hometown. Dressed in her black leather mini-skirt, black hose, high backless heels and white halter top, she bent, seductively, over the pool table attracting every male eye in the joint. Not only was she extremely available for the evening, she hadn't had any close bodily contact in several weeks and was feeling frisky, wanting everyone within glaring distance to know.

"Hi," said Andy Rhiland, a tall, good-looking rounder dressed in jeans and a white t-shirt, displaying enough muscle to fill two bodies.

"Hi yourself," said Jules. "Now don't tell me, you want me to shoot a game of pool with ya?"

"Yes ma'am," he said, behind flashing coal-black eyes.

"Well, let's get it on then."

It was three o'clock in the morning, as the cool air wafted through the pine trees outside Jules' apartment. She was half drunk, guiding her daddy's old Dodge he'd lent her, into the parking lot. It was just a stroke of bad luck for Andy that he'd picked Jules to hit on that night, and that she'd invited him home for the evening.

The inebriated couple stumbled and groped their way up the stairs to Jules' second floor apartment, unable to see the stranger with the Red Man hat crouching in the shadows at the top of the stairway. They laughed and kissed, unable to keep their hands off one another until they paused momentarily outside the apartment door. It was never determined how five bullets could have been fired into her heart and one into his head without anyone hearing the gunshots, but Jules and Andy died that morning, as the rain cleansed their filthy bodies.

It was just poor timing that Bill entered the small town of Redwood just as Jules' body was being prepared for autopsy.

Chapter 52

Johnny Stone sat staring into his PC monitor when the phone on his desk rang.

"Johnny, this is Tuck. One of the guys at Turbalinda Farm said he saw Franke working over at Keeneland last weekend."

"Would you recognize him?"

"No, but one of the grooms from Turbalinda would. What say I get them together and we pay a visit to Keeneland?"

"Sounds good to me. The sooner the better."

"Okay, I'll get everything together for tomorrow afternoon. Let's meet there behind the blacksmith shed at noon."

"Okay, see you then."

One has to visit Keeneland Race Track only once to believe that heaven truly exists and that a small corner of it remains nestled between horse farms along Versailles Road approximately six miles west of downtown Lexington.

As the clock struck twelve, Johnny Stone arrived at the Keeneland blacksmith shed, followed shortly by Tuck, and two farm hands, Jimmy and Ruben. The foursome discussed the situation for a few moments, then walked over toward the barn where Franke'd been seen.

"Why don't we split up? We can't let him see all of us together, it might spook him," said Tuck.

"Okay, Ruben and I'll go up near the front. Tuck you go to the right and Johnny, you take the left. Ruben, if you see him, give me a signal. Take your hat off and wipe your forehead," said Jimmy.

"What do we do then?" asked Johnny.

"Just make sure he doesn't get away. Ruben, you just ask him how he's doing. If he stops and talks to you, we'll just sort of close in around him."

Ruben, hands in his pockets trying to look inconspicuous, slowly made his way up to the front side of the barn crossing through the shedrow entrance, where he saw Franke working a stall near the end of the barn. Ruben quickly took off his hat and moped his brow, as he was told. Not wanting to cause a scene, he turned and entered the stall.

"Hey Franke, how's it going? Ain't seen you in a while."

Without returning the salutation, Franke quickly tried to run from the stall, but Ruben jumped in front of him, blocking his escape. By then it was too late, as Tuck, Jimmy and Johnny closed in around him.

"Now don't be afraid Franke, we're not gonna hurt ya. We just want to ask ya some questions, that's all," said Tuck, reassuringly.

Realizing he was not going to get away, Franke flopped down on the floor of the stall and buried his face in his hands.

"I, I knew it was gon, gonna happen. I ju, just knew it."

"Franke, did you have anything to do with this stillborn problem we're having?" asked Tuck.

"Yeah. I da, did. Bu, but I d, don't know mu, much."

"What happened?" asked Tuck, sitting down next to the hapless groom. "Just tell us in your own words."

"He t, told me th, that I would g, get five th, thousand d, dollars if I would sp, spray the n, n, noses of them stallions."

"Who, Franke?"

"J, Jeff. I m, mean Mr. F, Fairchild."

"What was in the nose spray?"

"I d, don't know. I n, never kn, knew."

Tuck rushed to the phone in the office at the center of the barn and phoned Gwen.

"Gwen this is Tuck. Have I got news for you."

"Hey there stranger. So, what's up?"

"I've found the guy who says he sprayed some kind of substance into the noses of the stallions we've got quarantined. He says that he was paid to do it, but he doesn't know what was in the spray."

"Do the horses match up? I mean did he tell you the right stallions?"

"He sure did. He pretty much named every single one."

"That means we really don't have a virus," said Gwen, gleefully. "That means it must have been sabotage. Say, can you meet me first thing in the morning?"

"Yeah, I can do that."

"Okay, in my office. Eight sharp."

Chapter 53

Meredith and Dr. Radabaugh had been reviewing the data on the infected mares when Gwen and Tuck stopped by his office. Seeing the look on Gwen's face, he excused himself and went out into the hall.

"Doctor Radabaugh, Mr. Flannery has some interesting news," said Gwen.

"Hello Mr. Flannery."

"How are you sir?"

"So, what have you got?"

"I've found the man who claims to have sprayed a substance into the nostrils of each of the stallions you have quarantined. He says he visited ten farms and sprayed some kind of nose spray into their nostrils."

Dr. Radabaugh couldn't believe his ears. His head filled with questions of how and what, realizing at once that they were not facing something God had made. Inviting them in he introduced Tuck and Gwen to Dr. Pehlagrem. With more questions floating in their heads than answers, the four began a discussion that seemed to have no boundaries.

"I believe I know where the nose spray was developed. But I don't know why," began Meredith. "I also believe I know who was involved with its development, and I should know much more within the next few days."

"You mean to tell me that someone developed a substance that could cause a foal to be stillborn?" asked an amazed Tuck.

"I know it sounds pretty far fetched, but that certainly may be what's happened here," said Meredith. "Fred, when was the first stillborn?"

"March time-frame. About the first of March."

"Mr. Flannery, this guy you've found. Did he indicate when he infected the stallions?" asked Meredith.

"Not exactly. But he sure knew which horses were

infected."

"If this is true, this could be genetic," said Gwen.

"That could be," said Meredith. "But we need more information. What do you think, Fred?"

Dr. Radabaugh had been in deep thought since the discussion began and, as though he were in a daze said, "Sure, that would be fine."

"Mr. Flannery," asked Meredith, "what's the man's name who sprayed the stallions?"

"I believe they called him Franke, but I'm not sure of his last name."

"Can you find out when Mr. Franke did his spraying?"

"I'll see what I can do," said Tuck.

"OK. Fine. I should know more when I talk to my partner tonight. He should be confronting the person we think developed this nose spray sometime today."

"You mean you know who did this?" asked Tuck.

"We know certain things that seem to point in a similar direction. But we're not prepared to make any accusations just yet."

"Okay, I'll call Gwen after I've talked to Franke," said Tuck. "Hopefully, he'll tell me when he sprayed the stallions."

Chapter 54

The light on the answering service in Meredith's hotel room was blinking, as she opened the door, indicating that someone had tried to call. But before she had time to replay the message the phone rang. Recognizing Bill's voice, she was immediately disappointed by his tone.

"Are you sitting down, Mere?" he asked.

"Hi honey. What is it?"

"Jules is dead."

Meredith felt the energy run out of her body, as the words she'd just heard began to sink in.

"Oh no. Oh no. Bill, no."

"Yeah. I can't believe it either. She was shot right outside her apartment."

Meredith had heard enough bad news in her life, and was no stranger to adversity, but hearing that one of her employees had been killed, really saddened her.

"What else did you find out?"

"Not much. She was shot five times, though. And all in the heart. I don't know the significance of that, but it sure sounds like she must have been running in a pretty hard crowd."

"That would be us, wouldn't it? I mean, we were her crowd."

"No, I mean with the prince and all. You know they were into something really bad."

"Well, I just feel terrible. Why didn't we do something?"

"Now Mere, you know we couldn't have prevented this."

"I'm not so sure. If I had only known, I could have

done something."

"She wouldn't have allowed that, Mere. You know that as well as I do."

Meredith, feeling alone and vulnerable, asked "So, what's next? When will I see you?"

"I'm going to attend the funeral and then go back up home for a few days to complete the divorce proceedings and then I'll fly down to Kentucky. Just a few more days."

"I don't know if I can wait that long."

"Yeah, me too. I'll call you tomorrow night. Just remember that I love you and keep your chin up," said Bill, as he hung up the phone.

Meredith spent the night thinking about Jules and how she had wanted to use the lab back in Karoumi as a place to be alone. A place to be alone to develop a Thoroughbred nose spray.

Unable to find anything in the Karoumi Equine Center lab that would implicate Jules and associate her with Kentucky's stillborns, Meredith wanted desperately to believe that Jules had nothing to do with the whole thing, but knew in her heart, that Jules was anything but innocent.

But why? What caused Jules to want to do this?

Bill, on the other hand, thought about Jules' past. He was never really sure about her character and especially why she'd dropped out of school. He remembered she told him she'd been accepted into the graduate program at Cornell University, but told him she'd dropped out to "get her head together." Reaching for the phone, he dialed the long distance information operator.

"What city, please?" asked the operator.

"Ithaca, New York," said Bill. "I'd like the number for the Dean of Admissions at Cornell University."

Chapter 55

The following morning Meredith sadly revealed to Dr. Radabaugh that the person she thought was responsible for the stillborn malady had been murdered.

"So, we may never find out what this thing is."

"No," said Meredith, shaking her head in disbelief.

"That's a shame. I just hope we've corralled all the infected animals."

"You know Fred, Gwen might have been right yesterday. She said it's probably a genetic disorder."

"Well, that sounds good, but I don't see how she could make that claim. I mean she doesn't have a shred of evidence."

"That's just it. There is no evidence. The stallions are the ones infected, yet it shows up in the offspring without harming either parent. What else could it be?"

Dr. Radabaugh allowed his slender frame to sink into his chair, cupping his chin in his hands. Having been under enormous stress for several months, he was tired and it showed.

"We'll never know," he said slowly.

"At least you've got the horses isolated. You can test them at your leisure. This could be a blessing in disguise, Fred."

"Meredith, are you interested in a job?" he asked, with an innocent look on his face?

"Hey, I'm not going back to the Gulf, if that's what you mean. So, I just might be interested in a job."

"You've always got one here. I hope you know that."

"Well thank you, Fred. You don't know how much I needed that."

Bill called Meredith at her hotel room that night and informed her that Jules had indeed been expelled from Cornell due to unethical practices.

"How on earth did you find that out?" she asked.

"I have friends in high places."

"I was offered a job today, what do you think about that? You think you could work here in Lexington?"

"I've always wanted to work in the Bluegrass."

"How's it going with your lawyer?"

"Haven't had a chance to talk to him yet. I'll see him tomorrow after the funeral."

"Did you get to see Jules' parents?"

"Yes I did. They're quite a bit older than I'd expected. I didn't mention anything though. No sense adding to their grief."

"Did you talk to the police? I mean about her, you know?" Meredith stopped short, realizing there was nothing to link Jules to the problems in Kentucky, hence there was nothing to link her to anything at all.

"Nope. I'm just going to attend the funeral, sign the divorce papers, and fly to Lexington and you, sweetie."

"I can't wait. You know that? I can't wait."

"It won't be long now. I'll be on the last Delta flight into Bluegrass Field tomorrow night. I think it gets in at 10:18, or something like that."

"You've just made my day, Bill. I'll be there."

They didn't solve the mystery surrounding the stillborns, nor had they been able to prevent Jules Weherner's murder, but Bill and Meredith knew that their future lay before them in ways neither had ever allowed themselves to imagine. Their hearts burned with a wondrous flame, fueled from residual passion left unattended due to years of misplaced attention and unheralded love.

Chapter 56

Johnny and Sam debated long and hard on whether to write a follow-up story about what looked like a conspiracy to destroy Kentucky's number one cash crop.

"I don't know," said Sam. "Maybe we should just let this one be."

"You know Sam, this may be a first, but I'm tending to agree with you. I mean, what good would it do? Those doctors know which horses were infected. Don't they? And I believe they've pretty much got their arms around it. Don't you?"

"Then just let the sleeping dogs lie. Let it just die out," said Sam.

"Yeah, but what if some other crackpot tries this and is successful? I mean don't we owe it to the public to expose the whole plan?"

"I think alot of that depends on what happens to that Wilson character. Hell, they ought to throw the book at him."

"Don't you worry, about that. I just hope he gets a fair trial before they hang him. It's sad though, he's just a stumble bum who got hung out to dry by the wrong people."

"Yeah, but can't you say that about most folks who break the law?"

"I don't know about that," said Johnny. "But I can sure say it about me. I mean, look who I have to work with. And every day too."

"Ha, you ought to get on your knees and thank that gal from the university. She's the one who saved those horses."

"Well, she wouldn't have known about it if it wasn't for me," said Johnny, with a smile on his face.

"Oh, aren't you the smug one? Well how 'bout you and me slipping out a little early today to watch the Cats practice?

Maybe you can bestow some of that wisdom of yours on them."

"Now you're talking. And it's about time too," said Johnny, reaching for his coat.

Chapter 57

Tuck sat drinking his morning coffee, reading the newspaper with a huge smile on his face. Just days earlier, he was justifiably scared that the Thoroughbred industry teetered on the edge of disaster, facing total collapse. Especially in Kentucky. Who knew how many horses would have had to be put down if the event were to continue its out of control path? It had been a rough ride for several in the business of raising race horses, and he was relieved beyond description that the animal, upon whose back his livelihood rested, was saved from what could have been a gloomy ending.

He thought about the happenstance of meeting a woman for whom he'd begun having feelings.

What if this didn't happen? he thought. *I'd never have met her. So, I guess every cloud has a silver lining of some sort.*

He thought of his father. *I guess it's best that you weren't here to see all this, Dad. It would probably have killed you.*

He was just about to start his daily work routine when he heard his phone ringing in the hall.

"Tuck this is Gwen."

"Hey lady. How's it going?"

"Great! Just wondering if you'd like to ride out to the Horse Park and look at the group?"

"Is that what you're calling them? The group?"

"Can't think of a a better name. Want to ride out there with me? I've got to run some tests."

"Sure. You gonna pick me up?"

"A man after my own heart. Tell you what. I'll be there in less than twenty minutes."

"And I'll be waiting."

The pin oak leaves danced about the trees lining the narrow roads surrounding the pastures of the Kentucky Horse Park. Out beyond the immediate fields where the work horses were kept, and not far from I75, in a large open field stood the group of infected mares grazing as though nothing had ever happened. Tuck and Gwen leaned over the fence to watch as the colorful group of dark bay, chestnut, black and gray mares wandered over toward them.

The serenity of the green grass, the wafting of the willow trees and horses' tails lazily flicking in the breeze, filled their hearts with the fact that the Thoroughbreds would continue grazing where the air would be fresh, the sun would shine bright, and their remaining days would be blessed by the protective hand of God.

Acknowledgments

I would like to express my appreciation to the following individuals who have blessed this work with their participation:

My wife, Judy, for laboring with me through the sleepless, endless nights.

Kara Johnson, whose input was significantly vital to the storyline.

Sharon Bradley, for her genius in developing the cover. She managed to capture the entire storyline in a single illustration.

Lorraine Layne, whose invaluable reviews and editing added much to the overall quality, especially in the early going.

Vanda Bates, for her colorful stories of horsemanship.

Patrick Francis Monahan, whose initial idea was significant.

www.ingramcontent.com/pod-product-compliance
Lightning Source LLC
Chambersburg PA
CBHW050532260626
47157CB00004B/1574